Metaphorosis

November 2020

Beautifully made speculative fiction

Also from Metaphorosis

Verdage

Reading 5X5 x2: Duets
Score – an SFF symphony
Reading 5X5: Readers' Edition
Reading 5X5: Writers' Edition

Metaphorosis Magazine

Metaphorosis: Best of 20xx
Metaphorosis 20xx: The Complete Stories
annual issues, from 2016

Monthly issues

Plant Based Press

Best Vegan Science Fiction & Fantasy
annual issues, from 2016

from B. Morris Allen:
Susurrus
Allenthology: Volume I
Tocsin: and other stories
Start with Stones: collected stories
Metaphorosis: a collection of stories

Metaphorosis

November 2020

edited by
B. Morris Allen

ISSN: 2573-136X (online)
ISBN: 978-1-64076-181-0 (e-book)
ISBN: 978-1-64076-182-7 (paperback)

Metaphorosis
a magazine of speculative fiction
from
Metaphorosis Publishing

Neskowin

Madam Savva's Magical Emporium

James Rumpel

There'd been a time, a couple of years ago, that Bobby's Diner would be jam-packed during the noon hour. Over half the customers would be cops, like me, grabbing a quick bite before heading back to their beat. That wasn't true any longer. On this rainy Friday, April 13th, the place was nearly empty. The counter only had one customer and that was Creepy Charlie, who always spent hours nursing a single cup of joe. All but three of the booths and tables were empty. The place was so deserted that no one minded when Archie Crumpfeld shouted to me from his table.

"So, Rheinhart, I'm surprised to see you here. Someone with your poor arrest standing can't afford to take any sort of break."

What he said was pretty much true. Since the municipal budget cuts had gutted the police department, the captain had started using an arrest quota. Any cop who didn't make the required number of arrests per month would likely find themselves laid off. Dozens of officers had been let go in the last year.

I'd been having a tough time myself lately. Not many cases broke my way, and when they did, other cops stepped in and made the arrests, stealing the credit. The captain's quota brought out the worst in many of my coworkers. It had gotten so bad that some were even falsifying evidence or planting drugs on innocent civilians. I'd never let myself do anything that unethical.

Of course, I couldn't give Crumpfeld the satisfaction of agreeing with him. "I'm doing just fine," was my reply.

"That's not what the tote board in the precinct says. According to that, you've only given a ticket to a jaywalker and nabbed a guy for removing the tag from a mattress."

"You're wrong," I replied. And he was. I hadn't arrested the tag remover. It turned out he had permission from the manufacturer.

"Last night," continued Archie, "I came close to catching the gang that's been doing the break-ins along Main Street. I would have had them if I didn't have to stop for an old woman crossing the street. Somehow, I lost their truck in traffic."

"Yeah, I heard about your near success from Bob Harris. He was telling everyone in the precinct that you stole his info and tried to jump his arrest. Harris was pretty mad."

"Hey, I'm just doing my job," said Crumpfeld. "I've got a wife and kids to support."

I just shrugged, not in the mood to talk with Archie any longer. I hoped he wouldn't be the one to finally capture the Main Street Robbers. For months, no one had been able to crack that case. Every time someone got close, the thieves would somehow manage to get away. There were even a few strange theories floating around that the gang was using some kind of magic, but I had a hard time believing that. Whoever did solve the case would get on the Captain's good side. That officer wouldn't have to worry about layoffs for a long time.

Archie kept talking, but I had turned my attention to Zelda, my waitress, as she brought me a fresh cup of coffee. She set down the cup and winked at me. We had been doing a little harmless flirting ever since she started working for Bobby a few months ago.

"Here you go, hon," she said, with a smile. She was beautiful, as always, even wearing the old-fashioned uniform Bobby made his waitresses use. Her hair was pulled back in a tight bun.

"So, how's your mother doing?" I asked.

"Thanks for asking. She's doing better. I think I'm going to have her keep staying with me, though. She just can't handle her big drafty house. It'll be good for her if I take care of her for a while." She grabbed a strand of loose hair and tucked it behind her right ear.

"What's with the hoop earrings?" I asked. "Don't you always wear those little ruby studs?"

Zelda laughed, "Boy Harry, you pay close attention to what I wear."

"No," I lied. "It's just that the ones you're wearing now don't bring out the color in your cheeks." I immediately regretted how stupid that must have sounded.

She didn't embarrass me, she just grinned and whispered, "Don't let Crumpfeld get you down. He's just a big mouth. So, you've hit a bad streak. Things will turn around."

Before I could thank her for the coffee and the support, Archie's gruff voice interrupted our moment.

"Hey, Zelda. I'd like some more coffee too."

Zelda turned toward Archie's table, her face redder than the ruby earrings she normally wore.

"You'll get yours soon enough, Officer Crumpfeld. Some things are more important than making an arrest. Harry cares about people." She turned and headed back to the kitchen.

A little surprised by her outburst, I watched her as she walked away. I sipped my coffee, enjoying the embarrassed look on Crumpfeld's face out of the corner of my eye.

I was taking another drink when my radio started beeping. I could hear Charlie's going off too. There was a local call coming in. Whoever took the call first would get to handle the situation and, maybe, get an arrest to put on the precinct tote board.

Panicking, I realized that my radio was still in my jacket, on a hook by the front door. I stood, fumbling with my wallet as I tried to pull out some cash to leave on the table. I could see Charlie's radio on the chair across from him. There was no way I was going to get to my radio before he got to his.

That is, until Charlie's arm knocked into the pot of hot coffee Zelda had just brought to him. She dropped the pot and coffee spilled all over his pants. He jumped to his feet, shrieking and trying to get the burning hot coffee off his legs.

Zelda, who was wiping off the table, smiled at me as I ran to my jacket.

I was already talking to the dispatcher when I squeezed past an old lady standing in the doorway, shaking rain from her open umbrella.

The call sent me to investigate a break-in at 1313B Gretel Avenue. By the time I got to the place, the rain had stopped. I sidestepped a couple of puddles on my way to the door of a Victorian brick home. The house was old and badly in need of repair. Most of the bricks were dirt-covered and cracked. Many of the roof's shingles were missing, making it look like a deformed checkerboard. Black shutters covered all the windows. To my surprise, the house number was 1313A. I looked for another entrance, and eventually noticed a small garden shed in the backyard with 1313B painted over the doorway.

It seemed odd for a tiny shed to have an address, let alone be a crime scene, but I had a job to do. I knocked on the door.

I had barely touched the wood when the door opened inward, creaking loudly. There was no one there except for a fat black cat. Staring in disbelief, I stepped into a large foyer that couldn't possibly have fit in the shed. The cat stopped after a few feet and looked back at me.

What was going on here? The place was way too large on the inside. The cat walked through an open interior doorway. The words MADAM SAVVA'S MAGICAL EMPORIUM glowed above the entrance. That couldn't mean actual magic, could it? I took another look around the foyer, took a deep breath, and followed the cat.

Past the doorway, I found myself face to face with a middle-aged woman wearing a black dress. The cat was nowhere to be seen.

"Thank you for coming so quickly. I am Madam Savva," she said. As I watched, she seemed to grow four or five inches taller and her hair changed from gray to red. She was now wearing a blue pantsuit.

I put my hand on a desk to steady myself, and stood there with my mouth wide open.

"I don't mean to scare you. I know you haven't been exposed to much magic. Please accept my apologies. I was in the middle of testing a transformation potion when you knocked on the door."

I had never believed the stories of magic users in the city. It always seemed too weird to be true. But now, seeing a woman transforming before my eyes, I couldn't help but accept the idea, much as I disliked it. I took another deep breath and tried to act normal.

"So, magic is real?" I asked, hoping the woman would tell me it was all some sort of parlor trick.

"Oh, very much so," replied the woman, now much shorter and with jet black, shoulder-length hair. "There are quite a few adepts living in the city. We try to keep as low a profile as possible. That's why this place is hidden in a shed and why I make the main house look so run down. We only make our presence known on rare and very important occasions. I think the last time I spoke about magic to non-adepts was at Woodstock, not that any of them would remember."

I still didn't know if I could accept what the woman was claiming. "I've been working the beat in this city for ten years. I would have met other witches by now."

Madam Savva's smile disappeared for a brief moment. "We prefer to be called adepts." The pleasant smile returned as quickly as it had left. "You have probably met many of us. Most adepts lead simple lives and work common, everyday jobs. They just happen to have the ability to use a little magic now and then."

"Most?" I asked.

"Well, yes," she answered. Her appearance had continued to shift throughout our conversation. At this moment she was a teenage girl with braces. "Some of us are more powerful," she continued, "and there are a few who use their skills in, shall I say, less acceptable ways."

"You mean to commit crimes?" My mind was racing. Not only was I trying to come to grips with the reality of magic, but I was also beginning to form a theory about how the Main Street Robbers consistently got away.

Madam Savva nodded. "Yes, that's why I have asked for your help. There's been a robbery." She spread her arms wide, showing me the room. "You see, this is my shop. I procure and sell all sorts of magical items. Some are very powerful and very dangerous. That's why many of my products have a ten-day waiting period."

I examined the room. The place was jam-packed with stacks upon stacks of all sorts of junk. Chests and boxes filled dozens of shelves. An entire corner was filled with cloaks and gowns. Each article of clothing floated as if hung on an invisible hanger. Another section of the room was filled with all styles of furniture; antique tables, modern lounge chairs, and large wardrobes were tightly packed together. An immense bookshelf filled the far wall. There had to be thousands of leather-bound books and dog-eared paperbacks on the shelves. The room was an utter mess, but an impressive mess.

I wondered if anything had actually been stolen. Maybe it was simply misplaced. It was hard to imagine anyone being able to keep track of everything in this place.

Whatever was going on, I needed to try and solve this case. "Well, let me get a full report from you. Let's sit down and discuss what happened." I walked over to a fancy dining set and took an old book off one of the chairs, making room to sit down.

"Oh, you don't want to sit there," she said. "You see that's a magic table. Anyone who sits in it becomes completely satisfied with their location and never wants to leave. It's called a Table of Contents." For a second, she looked confused.

"Okay, well how about that one?" I gestured toward a simple wooden table.

"No, you don't want to sit there either. If you sit there, you will be transported to some other time. The table will send you to a different era."

"That's amazing; a table that lets you travel through time. What do you call it?"

Madam Savva seemed to be fighting an internal struggle. She appeared to not want to answer me, but she did. "It's a

Periodic Table." She shook her head as if she were upset with herself.

"Well, is there anywhere we can sit?" I asked.

"Definitely not the Lazy Boy." Without another word, Madam Savva walked over to a desk and pulled a handful of purple and pink confetti from a drawer. She tossed the tiny papers in the air. While the pieces were floating to the ground and onto us, she shouted, "Pundunia."

"I'm sorry for that," she said. "The book you moved was the Book of Infinite Puns. You must have triggered it. We should be able to have a normal conversation now."

"Okay," I replied, "Let's just do this standing." By now the woman had stopped transforming and maintained the appearance of a thirty-some-year-old woman with curly brown hair. She had soft features and a tiny button nose. She didn't look anything like a witch.

"What was stolen?" I asked.

"Only one thing was taken. But it is very valuable and, if used, it could cause a lot of trouble. A Potion of Luck is missing."

"That doesn't sound so bad."

"You have no idea. If someone drinks too much of it, the entire infrastructure of society could be changed. Imagine someone having everything go their way. Businesses could collapse. People could die. Even if they don't mean for anything bad to happen, it still could. The potion doesn't care about collateral damage; it only brings the best possible luck to its user."

"If it is so dangerous, why do you even have it here?"

Madam Savva shrugged. "I used to sell it in very small portions, nothing more than a few drops. But then the Cubs won the World Series and I realized how unpredictable it could be. It's valuable enough that I don't want it destroyed. I keep it hidden in a drawer behind the counter."

"Are you sure it was stolen? Couldn't it have been misplaced?" I was beginning to fear that this case would be impossible for me to solve. I knew nothing about the magical world. I had no connections or inside information.

"No, it's gone. I have a very good system for keeping track of things. The fact that it was the only item taken points out that it was someone who not only knows about magic, but knows this place quite well. They wanted that specific item."

"Is there anyone you suspect? Has anyone asked about that potion lately?"

"Not that I know of. There were about a dozen customers in here yesterday. Whoever took it must be pretty good with cloaking spells. They've done a good job covering their tracks. If I could have figured this out on my own, I would have. I need your help." She didn't try to hide her frustration.

I looked around the cluttered room for any surveillance equipment. Not seeing any, I asked Madam Savva if the store had any.

"I'm afraid not," she said. "But we do have something just as good." She led me over to an old-fashioned easel. The pencil drawing on the top piece of parchment showed the two of us standing in front of an old-fashioned easel in a cluttered magic store.

"This is a magic easel," she explained. "It makes instantaneous drawings of its surroundings."

"I can see that."

"I just need to find a drawing from when the thief was in here." She started flipping through the pages, tossing sheet after sheet over the top. Suddenly she stopped. "Unbelievable. Whoever stole the potion must have torn off the pages with their image on them." She pointed to the small bits of paper where those drawings had been. "We'll never be able to find out who did it. What a rip-off."

I tried my best to console her. "I promise to do the best I can. There are some things I can try. I'll leave no sheet unturned. Oh, and I think your anti-pun spell is wearing off."

We looked at the drawings of the previous day's visitors, and I had Madam Savva tell me as much as she could about each of them. Afterward, I headed out to start my investigation. When I reached the street, I stopped in my tracks. Someone had let the air out of all four of my car's tires and broken the side mirrors.

The dispatcher had a good laugh at my expense and told me that she'd send someone to fix the tires, but it would take at least an hour for them to get there. I decided I might as well look around the neighborhood; maybe there was a clue to be found somewhere around the magic shop. Besides, I could use the time to try and wrap my mind around everything I had seen in Madam Savva's store.

I was walking by a large grocery store when a produce truck came out of the loading dock and headed up the street. As it turned, a large crate of bananas fell off the back and crashed on the pavement. Bananas flew everywhere, but the driver was long gone before I could try to wave him down.

I was bending down to pick up a banana when I heard voices coming from the other side of the wooden fence around the loading dock.

"I've got nearly a hundred of these TV sets," said a man with a thick Irish accent. "If you give me two hundred bucks each, you can have them all."

"Well, it looks like a nice set," said the other voice, "but I'd have to ship them to another city to sell them. I'm willing to pay one hundred per TV."

I crept to the open gate and peeked around the corner. In the dimming light, I recognized Dimples McGruder holding a large television. McGruder was well known to all the police officers in the city. He'd been running all sorts of cons, schemes, and heists for years.

Quietly, I pulled out my gun. I was going to get him this time. I had him red-handed.

Jumping out from behind the fence, I began to shout, "You're und..." Before I could finish, my foot came down on one of the many bananas laying on the ground. In Saturday morning cartoon fashion, I slipped and fell, tumbling into a pallet of table-salt containers. A dozen blue canisters fell on my head, spilling salt everywhere.

McGruder and his buyer took off in opposite directions. I tossed a handful of salt over my left shoulder and started after McGruder.

I followed him down a back alley, quickly gaining on him. McGruder was not very fast and the television he'd held onto didn't help him. Despite my earlier tumble, I was going to make this arrest.

We were on the thirteen hundred block of Gretel Avenue when I got close enough to shout, "Stop! You're under arrest." To my surprise, McGruder skidded to a halt in front of Madam Savva's magic shed.

I was just starting to sprint the last few yards when I felt a sharp pain on the ball of my right foot. It felt as if I'd been stabbed by a very small but very sharp knife. My next step was just as painful. When I tried to not put any weight on that foot, I lost my balance.

When I stumbled, McGruder shrugged and took off again.

With each step, the pain got worse. Slowly but surely, McGruder pulled further and further ahead of me. Eventually, I lost him. From an adjacent street, I heard the sound of a large truck stopping and restarting, but I couldn't see the vehicle or the direction it took.

Frustrated, I took a seat on the door stoop of a rundown apartment building, about five blocks from my car. I took off my right shoe and pulled out a tiny red ear stud. For a while, I just stared at the little ruby, thinking about what it meant.

The earring had gotten into my shoe while I was running by the magic emporium. Had Zelda been to the magic store? She hadn't been on any of the drawings, but the thief had removed some of the pictures.

This day just kept getting worse and worse. Was the one case I had a chance to solve going to require me to arrest the only person who seemed to want to be my friend?

With a sigh, I stood and took out my car keys. The way the day was going, it was no surprise that I dropped them. They landed in a rosebush growing under a ladder which leaned against the building. Cursing silently, I got down on my hands and knees and began feeling around for the keys.

The sound of a large truck stopping in front of the building caught my attention. I didn't want to stand up too fast and hit my head on the ladder, so I stayed hidden behind the bush. Soon, I heard voices.

"Tommy, you start unloading the goods," said a familiar voice with an Irish brogue. "Put them in the garage with the other stuff. I'll call a different buyer and set up a meeting."

"I don't want to do it myself," replied a voice that I assumed belonged to Tommy. "Those TV's are heavy. Why don't you help me first and then call the fence?"

"Okay. Okay," said the first man. "We have to hurry; the truck's invisibility spell will be wearing off soon and that cop might still be wandering around."

Pulling out my gun again, I waited another minute and then popped up from behind the bush. Dimples McGruder and another black-clad man stood in front of me, each holding a large color television.

"Freeze," I shouted. "You're under arrest."

Both men looked around, trying to find a way to escape. Before either could make a move, a black sedan squealed to a stop nearby. The police captain jumped out of the driver's seat.

"What's going on here?" he asked, glancing at me as he moved toward the two criminals.

"I just nabbed the Main Street Robbers," I said.

The captain grinned. "Very nice work, Rheinhart. I'll help you take them in. It was lucky I decided to take the long way home tonight."

After an evening filling out arrest reports, I had to confront Zelda. The next morning, I waited in the diner's parking lot.

"I know what you did," I said when she got there. "You took the luck potion from Madam Savva." I opened my hand to show her the ruby earring.

"Congratulations, Harry," she said, not admitting anything. "I hear you got lucky with an arrest."

"It wasn't lu…" The realization hit me like a ton of bricks. "You gave me the luck potion."

"Just a drop in your coffee. I knew how bad things were going for you. I heard Crumpfeld giving you a hard time every day."

I'd always been a good cop. I played by the rules, and I knew I should arrest Zelda. After all, she had committed a crime. But how could I turn her in? She had stolen the potion to help me.

"Do you still have the potion? Did you use it for anything else?"

"I have it in my purse. I just…" She smiled and shrugged. "I thought it was worth the risk to help a friend, but that's the only time I used it."

"But you are a wi… an adept"

Zelda shrugged. "Not really. My mother helped me get the potion."

She reached into her purse and pulled out a jar filled with a moldy-looking, green liquid. "Here's the potion. Do what you have to."

The more I thought about it, the more I realized I couldn't arrest her. It was because of the stolen potion that I'd caught the Main Street Robbers. I didn't think the captain would understand. How would he react to the idea of magic? Would he even give me credit for either arrest?

"Okay. Here's what's going to happen. I am going to take this back to Madam Savva. I'll tell her the thief was lucky enough to get away." I had to smile. "I think it'll be believable. But you have to promise to never do anything like that again."

Her smile assured me that I had made the right choice. "Of course not. Though I wouldn't mind if you found the time to keep a little closer eye on me." She pulled a pad and pen from her apron and wrote down a phone number. "I'd like it if you called me and set up a little reconnaissance."

I couldn't keep myself from grinning. "Maybe we could go see a movie or something. The captain gave me tonight off."

Zelda flashed a sly smile. "Well, isn't that lucky? I get off at six."

See James Rumpel's story "Madam Savva's Magical Emporium" online at Metaphorosis. If you liked it, leave a comment. Authors love that!
Remember to subscribe to our e-mail updates so you'll know when new stories are posted.

About the story

"Madam Savva's Magical Emporium" was written at the end of March 2020. There were a lot of strange and unprecedented things happening in our world at that time, most of them negative. I had friends and family who were struggling with fear and adjusting to quarantine. My goal was to write a positive, upbeat tale to remind myself and everyone else that sometimes good things happen to good people. I wanted to create a story about someone having unexpected good fortune and I think I was lucky enough to come up with an interesting way for that to happen.

Once I started writing, the story took shape fairly quickly, especially when I found a way to work in a little word play. I love puns and was ecstatic that I could sneak in a few within the confines of the story.

I write because it's fun, and I had a good time putting this piece together. I hope others will enjoy it also.

A question for the author

Q: Whence do you draw inspiration for your characters?

A: To be honest, most of my stories begin with a plot and then the characters just show up. I guess I have a vast collection of characters to choose from. Having taught high school for thirty-four years, I've worked with thousands of students, parents, and coworkers. Additionally, I have avidly read and watched movies and television most of my life. There are all sorts of people in my mind trying to push their way into my stories.

About the author

James Rumpel is a retired high school math teacher who has enjoyed spending some of his additional free time trying to turn some of the strange ideas filling his brain into stories. He lives in Wisconsin with his wonderful wife, Mary.

The Preserved City

Charles Schoenfeld

Simona's view of the modern city dropped away as the cable car rose toward *Città Alta*. Above the ancient city wall, she could see black-clad families milling about in the pre-dawn glow. Services would begin in twenty minutes, at 5:00 a.m. Those who had risen early were enjoying the beauty of the upper city, its medieval architecture and narrow cobbled streets unaltered since Renaissance times.

Simona's black shawl rubbed against her lips, and she brushed it away. She had been awake longer than any of her neighbors. In Bergamo—or any northern city—the women did not prepare feasts on

All Souls' Day, nor leave their homes open for the spirits. But Simona kept up the southern traditions, even if her grandmother would have cringed to see her preparing portions of that feast in the microwave.

The funicular deposited Simona near the Piazza Vecchia. The other women greeted her warmly as she crossed the square. They asked about her work, which made it necessary to lie. "Making progress," she said.

Two years earlier, most of them had come to see *L'Applauso È Napoletano* in its first few weeks at La Scala. They were not habitual opera-goers, but they knew the composer and took neighborly pride in her success.

It was an easy story for northerners to love. While her opera gave an inevitably nostalgic, romanticized view of Campania, her southern home, it was ultimately a paean to everything Bergamo had taught her to love about the north: its scenic beauty, its air of civilized contentment. The southern heroine does not *return* home in the end; she *finds* home.

Every line of the square's architecture drew Simona's eyes upward—the arches and pillars of the library's white façade, the stony bulk of the ancient bell tower. An archway led to the chapel. Simona found a seat near its acoustic center. Stefano, her fiancé, would be attending services with his family in Milan, an hour away. He had invited her, but she had a plan of her own for this morning, and it could only be accomplished here, in the Basilica of Santa Maria Maggiore.

Simona joined her neighbors in lighting candles for the departed and reciting the prayers. Some of the women who had lost relatives within the past year wept while the organ played.

Simona's analytical facility had outgrown its proper place in her mind. She did not hear the organ music as a unified whole; her ear picked the musical phrases apart into individual chords, and the chords into isolated notes. This rendered the composition meaningless; any arbitrary substitution could have been made, and would neither improve nor damage the music.

A-flat? Why not G?

Half note? Why not two quarter notes?

Composer's intuition, she answered herself. *I used to have it too.*

The mass ended. While the other churchgoers dispersed to tend family graves, Simona made her way to the rear of the church, where lay the one dead Bergamasco to whom she felt any connection.

Simona knew of no more touching monument, anywhere, than the relief carved on Donizetti's tomb. It depicted a group of cherubs at the moment when they heard of the composer's death. Several were bending and breaking their lutes; one, angry-faced, held his lute over his head with both hands, ready to smash it upon the ground; another stood poised to crush his lute beneath his upraised foot. In the center of the relief, a kneeling cherub wept, hands covering his face, while the cherub at left gazed heavenward in despairing incomprehension.

Simona traced the relief with her fingertips, then began to speak.

From its long rest, Gaetano Donizetti's consciousness flickered into existence, so that a sound might intrude upon it. A woman's voice said, "… to pay respect to you on this day."

Inside the tomb, Donizetti's soul formed a vague head-shape and nodded it in recognition. The living often stopped by to honor his memory. On All Souls' Day, when the barrier between worlds was thinnest, he could hear them.

"Great master, offer me guidance—"

Guidance? There was a dangerous word. She hadn't fallen to her knees before his tomb, had she? His senses sharpened; he tried to be certain.

"I have succeeded once. And now, no music I write approaches the beauty of what I've already written. But you, you breathed music as others breathe air—"

Excessive flattery. I worked at my music.

"Teach me to remember what I once knew. Help me to release the music in my soul—"

He formed a face, which formed a scowl. *I joined the army rather than teach music. Know me before you ask these things.*

Her voice was growing ever more frantic. "Don't leave me in this state: silent, unheard. I exist for Music—"

No, no, this is all wrong. An ember of outrage began to glow in the dark of Donizetti's tranquility. *Music should give joy to its creator, never enslave her. Else, why create?*

"Inhabit me, if you can." Her voice was choked. "Make me your instrument. If I can no longer create, I can still ... I can ..."

Must you make me care for you? There should be peace in death.

"I'm sorry, I don't know what I'm saying. Forgive me."

Pity overcame Donizetti at last, if only by a narrow margin. He gathered himself and stepped from his tomb, but there was no one kneeling before it.

Footfalls echoed on the flagstones. He caught the barest glimpse of her flushed, tear-streaked cheek as she ran from the chapel. But today, on All Souls' Day, he could be anywhere within *Città Alta*, instantly. Anywhere that he had been before. So, the barest glimpse would be enough.

Simona walked the narrowest of the old streets, turning her face to the walls until she had composed herself enough to be seen without loss of dignity. She descended to *Città Bassa* via the funicular and went home.

Stefano arrived that evening. His gaze lingered on the feast she had left for the spirits. She'd been composing, and had not yet cleaned it up.

Stefano had advised against leaving her home open all day, but now he refrained from comment. She loved him for all the protective things he obviously wanted to say, and loved him even more for having enough respect not to say them.

She cleared away the dishes and prepared a dinner. While they ate, Stefano told her stories about his family, with whom he had spent the day. His younger sister had a new boyfriend, of whom Stefano did not quite approve. Simona found it adorable that his protective tendencies applied to everyone he loved, not only to herself.

Stefano's older sister worked as an assistant manager in a hotel. She always had hilarious, and sometimes infuriating, stories about the guests, which Stefano recounted in as much detail as he could remember.

For Simona, whose thoughts of late had revolved entirely around her music and how little of it she was writing, Stefano's willingness to carry the conversation came as a welcome diversion. She could forget her concerns for a while, as he chattered on.

Then, for an instant, they were not alone at the table. One of the empty chairs was occupied by a ... trick of the light. But it was a man-shaped trick, with a wild curl of shadow atop its head and another that might have been a bow tie beneath its chin. When she turned to glance at it, one of its eye-shimmers disappeared and reappeared. On a more solid form, it might have been a wink. Then the figure vanished.

"Are you all right?" Stefano asked, breaking off in the middle of a story.

"Hmm?"

He smiled. "You went away for a minute there."

He hadn't seen it, then. "Oh, sorry. I was just wondering ... can you stay the night?" She picked up her empty plate and carried it into the kitchen.

He followed with his own plate. "I hadn't planned on it, but I'd love to. You know I have to wake up early for work?"

"I know. It's just ... there's something a little spooky about this holiday, isn't there? The spirits of the departed walking around? Your presence would be comforting."

She didn't want to tell him what she had seen. For one, she wasn't certain she had seen it. And even if she had, Stefano tended to worry when she had a problem he couldn't solve, or wasn't supposed to.

"And your presence would be delightful," he replied. He kissed her, and she kissed back, made it last longer than he had planned, turned his casual gesture into one full of longing and love.

"Yours too," she said. "Especially if you can get up for work without waking me."

"I'll do my best."

During breakfast the next morning, alone in her apartment, Simona put on her recording of *L'Applauso*. She had not listened to her own work in months. She had polished it so lovingly, and they had found the ideal performer for every role. The recording had captured her music the way it was *supposed* to sound. It made anything different—anything new—seem wrong. She worried that her next work would sound like a soulless imitation of her one great success. That was the easiest thing for reviewers to write about *any* composer's second offering. They almost didn't need to attend a performance.

So instead, Simona's new work accumulated in her wastebasket over the course of each day. Soulless imitation might be an improvement.

She sorted through piles of CDs. *Mozart ... Rossini ... trick of the light.*

There he was, depicted on the cover of a CD. The same wild curl of hair she had perceived as a shadow. Not a bow tie, but a cravat. Donizetti. And he had winked at her.

She rushed from the apartment without finishing breakfast.

All Souls' Day had passed, and the barrier between worlds had begun to thicken. Normally, it would have taken enormous energy for Donizetti to travel the city freely —the sort of energy that comes from unresolved grievances against the living. Donizetti had no unfinished business, but now he had a connection to a mortal.

They had kept his old bed, all these years. It was on display in his museum, a small, second-floor suite of rooms that also housed his sheet music, instruments, clothing, and other personal effects.

He knew that the woman would come. She had asked for him, and he had appeared. It had taken all of his concentration to make himself visible in *Città Bassa*, even just barely visible, even just for a moment. But he had done it, and she would come.

His old doublet hung on a wooden tailor's dummy. He touched it, let his fingers pass through the velvet, let the feel of it come alive in his memory. Then, with a moment's concentration, he shaped the matter of his soul to resemble it. He repeated the trick with his old walking stick, touching the original and creating a spirit replica that he could hold.

So he lay on his old bed, wearing his old finery, one sole planted on the mattress, his knee pointed jauntily upward. He twirled the walking stick in his fingers, and he waited.

The woman arrived flushed and panting. There was something tentative about the way she walked, the way her eyes traced each surface, wondering if it might be inhabited by a spirit, if ghosts really could exist and answer people's prayers.

When she saw Donizetti, she froze for a moment, taking in the sight of him. She swallowed. "It *was* you," she said. "You came to me."

"And you," Donizetti replied, his nasal voice resonating off the walls, "took your time returning the favor!"

He sprang from the bed in one fluid motion, rapped his walking stick twice on the floor. "Come! We have work to do."

In Florence, which had been home to Leonardo and Michelangelo for long portions of their lives, Donizetti might have been dimly remembered, a historical footnote. In the quiet mountain town of Bergamo, he was the most renowned of the city's sons, the single greatest source of civic pride. One could not spend much time in Bergamo without hearing his name. That was one reason Simona had chosen him to hear her prayer.

Still, praying to the great man's tomb had been one thing. Sharing his company, bearing the weight of his full attention, was another, and far more exhilarating.

"Begin by showing me how you compose," Donizetti said.

"What … what do you mean?"

"I mean, here is pen! Here is paper! Begin!"

Simona wondered how long their privacy would last. "What about …" She gestured toward the ticket-taker in the hallway, her back to the museum's entrance.

"These rooms are my domain. She will not hear what I do not wish her to hear. Now, begin."

Simona stood over an exhibit case, drew a staff on the blank page, hummed a few notes, and wrote them down. She ran a hand through her long hair, blew out a breath. Then she wrote a few more notes.

Donizetti stood at her shoulder, watching the pen move.

She paced the length of the main room once, twice. She picked up Donizetti's old violin. Conveniently, the museum kept it strung for appearance's sake. She gave it a cursory tuning, carefully played a few notes on it, and wrote them down. Then she snatched up the paper in one hand. She would have crumpled it, but hesitated, not sure whether she had permission.

The first ruined sheet of the day had come even faster than usual, with Donizetti watching.

He sighed theatrically. "I see. You know quite well *how* to compose. I am not so sure you remember *why*. Come, then." He swept out of the museum. The ticket-taker showed no awareness of him as he passed, but nodded to Simona as she followed.

In the Via Gombito, the ever-present Roaring Old Man tottered by, emitting nonsensical syllables and daring anyone to meet his gaze. He was a fixture in the afternoons; Simona encountered him nearly every time she visited *Città Alta*. "Arrrrhh!" he yelled, and, "Aiieeeee!" He tottered on his way. Donizetti leaned close to Simona and spoke in her ear. "A comic buffoon?" he suggested. "A drunken, declaiming baritone? Or a fallen genius—a strident tenor, lamenting his lost glory? Perhaps a spy, concealed in plain sight? The stuff of opera, in any case. *Compose him.*"

At the fortress called La Rocca, atop a broad tower of sand-colored stone, a stiff wind flapped the Italian flag. Donizetti stood in the center of the stone courtyard and shouted over the wind: "A mighty fortress! A symbol of liberty!" He stepped closer to Simona, lowered his voice. "But it was also a prison, once. And the French used it when they conquered us, and the Austrians too. There is music here. Stirring, patriotic music, and dark, oppressive music."

Simona looked at the fortress, trying to make the music come, but it would not come. She avoided meeting Donizetti's gaze, fearing to admit that she could look at La Rocca and hear nothing.

"Come," said Donizetti.

They climbed the bell tower and looked down into the Piazza Vecchia. Donizetti offered no commentary, seeming to wait for something. As Simona turned to face him, the huge bell tolled, just meters above her head. Donizetti flickered translucent and vanished. The sound took away Simona's ability to think, to descend the stairs, to do anything but cringe, hands over her ears, and wait for the bell to finish.

Finally she descended the tower and found Donizetti waiting. "You looked like you could use a shaking," he said. Simona stared at him in blank amazement, then laughed. Her eyes closed and her chest shook and as the tension left her, she realized it was the first time she had smiled in Donizetti's presence.

They walked along the city wall that divided the upper and lower parts of Bergamo. Simona wondered how *Città Bassa* must look to Donizetti, with its automobiles, with people tapping at their smartphones, skateboarders with their blue spiked hair, chemical plants and apartment complexes made of concrete, glass, and steel. Here stood one of Bergamo's most celebrated ancestors, surveying what his grandchildren's grandchildren had made of themselves. How would he judge it all?

She tried to put the question into words, but the thoughts seemed too large, and the words came out awkward, incomplete.

"I've never thought about it," Donizetti said.

They stopped and leaned against the wall, looking out over the valley. "Behind each window, along every street," said Donizetti, gesturing broadly across the expanse of orange-tiled rooftops that stretched all the way to the mountains, "a life runs its course. All of those lives, orbiting one another like planets, twinkling in isolation like the stars … and finally, scattered like dust." He blew on his upturned palm. "Compose *them.*"

"Have you done anything other than compose today?"

Simona jumped, her pen making a streak across her sheet music. She hadn't heard Stefano enter the apartment. "No, not today," she said. "Today was a composing day."

"It looks like it's been a composing *week.*" He started making a circuit of her apartment, picking up her discarded clothing from the backs of chairs, the couch, the floor, the dining table where she now sat working. He carried the clothing into her bedroom.

"You don't have to do that," she called after him.

"Which makes it wonderfully generous of me, don't you think?" He returned, gave her a quick smile that was probably supposed to be charming, and picked up a few of her discarded coffee mugs. He swept off to the kitchen.

Simona turned her attention back to her music. She tapped her pen against the table, trying to focus on the rhythm. Clattering dishes broke through her concentration, as Stefano began washing the ones she'd left in the sink. She stood and went into the kitchen.

"Was I expecting you tonight?" she asked.

"No. But your friend Donna called me and asked if you were all right. I told her I'd check on you."

"Donna called you?"

"She tried calling *you*, last night."

"I know. I wasn't answering the phone. I was—"

"Apparently it was her birthday? And you were invited to the—"

"Oh, *damn*. That was last night."

"It was."

"Great. That's fantastic." She stared at the ceiling for a moment. "Okay. I'll have to make it up to Donna, after I'm done with all this."

"Done with all what?"

"Finding my way through this ... this darkness in my mind. The music still isn't coming. It's not like writing *L'Applauso*. That's probably good. I'm not trying to write the same opera over again. But if

L'Applauso had failed, no one would have noticed. And if this fails, *everyone* will notice."

"People seem to notice when you forget their birthday parties, too." He gave a little chuckle, as if trying to make a joke of it.

"I know. I know what I owe my friends. But I know what I owe my audience, too. And I'm afraid, Stefano. It may be that what I owe them"—she tapped at her breastbone—"isn't in me anymore. What then? What am I supposed to do?"

"Well, I think you could start by taking a breath or two," he said. "Go for a walk, get some fresh air, have a nice meal. The audiences aren't demanding anything right now. You're the one putting all this pressure on yourself."

"No, of course the audience isn't demanding anything. And they won't. Audiences are always willing to forget you ever existed."

"I don't think they'll forget about you in the time it takes to … I don't know … go out for some gelato. Or go to a birthday party when you're invited."

"That's your solution to all this? Gelato?"

"Gelato is the solution to many of life's problems."

Simona rolled her eyes.

"I know it helps me when I'm having a hard time at work," he said.

"It's different for you. You leave the lab at the end of the day, and your work stays behind. It's just something you do; it isn't *who you are*."

"This isn't who you are, either," he replied. "This is a downward spiral. Look at this place. You're not taking care of yourself, you're not eating well ..." He opened one of her cupboards and removed a package of penne. "Let me cook you a nice dinner—"

She took the package from his hand. "Look, Stefano," she said. "You'll be a good father someday, but don't practice on me. I'm not a child."

"That's not what I—"

"And I don't think I'm hungry tonight." She replaced the penne on the shelf and closed the cabinet. "And I ... I don't think I'm in the mood for company. You should go."

"Simona, you *need* to—"

"Please go."

They stood facing each other for a long moment, each staring at a different spot on the kitchen floor, not moving except for the heaving of their chests as they breathed. Finally, Stefano left the kitchen. A moment later, Simona heard her front door open and close.

She returned to her dining table and began again to compose.

Donizetti took to unlocking his museum for Simona after the building had closed for the night. He never had to wait long for her to arrive. He insisted on candlelight, and on working long past midnight.

"Working through your fatigue will force your inhibitions aside," he said.

"Couldn't I just drink a bottle of wine?"

"No. Artists deprive themselves of sleep. Poseurs drink."

Città Alta had been wired for electricity, but he refused to permit its use while composing. *We must give you an authentic experience, after all,* he thought. *You believe that music must be a struggle. Let us take that belief to its extreme, and see what we may find there.*

"There is no music in these electric lights," he told her, his footsteps echoing in the silence of his museum as he slowly paced. "They don't flicker; they don't dance." He noticed a gutter of wax forming. "They don't weep. They only buzz, steady and atonal. We must surround ourselves with music, and weed out that which is not music."

Simona dropped her head back to the page in front of her and filled a few more measures.

Donizetti had learned to sneak glimpses at the music; Simona could not work while he stared. *Her music is beautiful*, he thought, watching her with sympathy. *Almost as good as mine.* He stepped closer to her and peered down his nose at her current score.

Perhaps better.

She had taken a modern office worker as her heroine. Her introductory scene was ambitious, panoramic. It began with an alarm clock, followed the young woman out of bed, through the horns-and-tubas rush of morning traffic, and into an office building. Percussion imitated the clack of computer keys, the clink of tiny espresso cups against saucers and desktops; strings toyed with the repetitive swoosh of a photocopier, the monotone flickering of fluorescent lights; a chorus of voices brought in the chaos of many distinct telephone conversations. Remarkably, the elements all blended, forming a unified impression that somehow gained in beauty the more hectic it became.

Donizetti stood dumbstruck. She had found the rhythm of her own world, the hidden melodies in those very aspects of modern life he had called devoid of music.

The heroine switched on her computer. Simona wrote: "Sintetizzatore"—synthesizer—then crossed it out, then began to write it again. She gave a cry of disgust, hammered her fist on the desk three times, and snatched up the paper. She crumpled it in one hand and threw it in the trash.

"Well, try again," was all Donizetti said. Encouragement might have helped her, but not in the way she needed.

She stayed there through the night and into the morning, composing and destroying, and did not leave Donizetti's rooms until nearly midday, as the museum began to receive its first visitors.

Donizetti followed her, to her surprise. "Not to worry," he said. "A change of scenery may do you good. Find a rock to sit on. Compose out here. There are no instruments here, but you can whistle."

She turned around to face him, staggering with fatigue. "Please, I need a break."

Donizetti nodded solemnly. *Then I shall break you.*

"All right," he said. "Follow me."

He led her to a restaurant and watched her order a margherita pizza. While she waited for her food, Donizetti stood over one of the other patrons, leaned in close and sniffed at her cappuccino. The woman seemed oblivious.

"Mmm," he murmured to Simona. "Such dark beauty in the scent of coffee. One forgets it as the decades pass. It entices you with its aroma, makes you feel strong even while wearing away at your insides. It is the most dangerous of lovers: the Seductress and the Destroyer. Soprano, perhaps? But slow and sultry in her rhythms. Even in coffee, there is music."

Simona was only half listening. Now that she had stopped moving, stopped working, hunger and fatigue threatened to consume her. The thought of coffee was tempting, but she needed solid food more urgently. Her skin felt tight on her bones, and the ambient sounds had taken on a tinny quality—not much bass, lots of treble.

The pizza arrived. Donizetti stood behind Simona's chair; he bent to position his lips behind her ear. "Good," he whispered. "Now a bite of pizza. Don't rush it. Taste the sunlight that shone on those tomatoes, the wood that fired the crust, the vitality of fresh basil. Yes."

Simona bit off a chunk of the pizza.

"Oh," said Donizetti, sounding rapturous. "In pizza one can taste all the bounty of nature, the benevolence of God. It is life's goodness in microcosm.

"Now: don't eat it. *Compose* it."

Simona's head snapped around to stare at him in horror. "Don't eat—?"

"You have tasted it once. Don't dilute the memory of that first taste."

But I'm so hungry.

Donizetti was relentless: "Feed your music first. You can feed your body afterward."

She stared at the slice of pizza in her hands.

Donizetti straightened from his crouch and looked down his nose at her, ready to issue his ultimatum. "Is this where I belong? You are not the only composer in Bergamo."

He turned away, took a step.

Simona leapt from her chair, reaching after him with both arms. "Wait! Don't go!" Her voice echoed off the nearby buildings.

He felt her fingertips pass through the velvet of his doublet and continued walking.

Behind him, Donizetti heard a small crowd detaining Simona, asking her if she felt all right. They could not see him; they would think she had been shouting and clawing at empty air. He allowed himself to fade from her view. Let her reassure them as best she could.

Only after she felt that she had hit some sort of a bottom could they attempt the real work of building her back up.

The crowd would have put her in the hospital if they'd had the power; Simona could see it in their faces. But she never asked for help, so eventually, they had to disperse.

Donizetti, when she found him again by the city wall, had softened somewhat. He looked her up and down as she approached, then said, "You may be right. You need to untwist yourself. Perhaps I have been too strict, depriving you of other composers' music all these weeks. Let your man take you to a concert tonight. Verdi is playing at the Teatro

Donizetti, and he is … competent. Enjoy yourself."

Donizetti vanished, his body distorting inward toward his own navel and shrinking to nothing. Simona wasn't sure, but she thought she heard a popping noise.

Space twisted around itself, and Donizetti felt himself spiraling through it, as if down a drain. Something had him by the soul. He hoped Simona could not tell that his disappearance had been unintentional. He hoped immortal souls could not be destroyed.

He hoped this was not what it felt like if they were.

He appeared with his back to his own tomb in Santa Maria Maggiore, contained by a half-circle of candles. He looked at the priest first, and did not recognize him. The man next to the priest, though, was Simona's lover, Stefano. They both held crucifixes.

"I saw you," Stefano said without preamble.

Donizetti made no reply.

"I saw Simona from below, walking along the city wall with another man one night," he said. "I wondered who you could be. Then her head eclipsed the moon—and yours didn't. The moon shone through your head. I knew immediately. What other spirit than you would she have chosen as her companion?"

"I am not a rival to you," said Donizetti. "I have no desire to—"

"She is unraveling. You had one full lifetime in which to compose. She is not your opportunity to live again."

The priest was chanting softly behind Stefano. Donizetti felt himself being pulled toward the inside of the tomb. The pull was soft, but getting stronger.

"She is an independent soul," Stefano continued, trembling with fury, "not a conduit for you to reclaim your—"

"She is dying," Donizetti said.

That stopped Stefano for a moment. Donizetti could see the doubt in his eyes: *Have we drifted so far apart that I would be the last to know?* Then he stood straighter, as if preparing to close a door in Donizetti's face. "No. She would have told me."

"Not her body," said Donizetti. "But you must have seen it by now." He tried to step forward out of the circle of candles, but met an invisible wall.

"Yes, I have. I've seen her obsessed by work as never before. An obsession to which *you* must have incited her. I've seen her neglecting her health, her friends—"

"Spare me," Donizetti spat. "She's told me of your great concern for her social obligations."

"Is that so?" Stefano's voice dropped to an injured whisper. "Because she's told *me* nothing of you."

"I can't imagine why not. You show such understanding of the work that's important to her."

Stefano turned his face away sharply, as if presenting the other cheek for Donizetti to strike. "Don't presume to judge me," he said. He met the composer's gaze again, his eyes glistening. "You may see her only as a musician. I see her as a whole person. I love her. And her friends, they love her."

"Then tell me: how much love do you think she could give to her friends if she had none left for herself?"

Stefano opened his mouth to reply, and closed it again.

"I would never deny the importance of friends and family," said Donizetti. "Nor do I doubt that they would provide shoulders for her to cry on, as she mourned the death of the music within her. But would they—would you—rather have a Simona who weeps on your shoulders, or one who stands proud, full of life, full of joy?"

"I have not seen that Simona since you arrived on the scene, *Signore*."

"You lost her before I arrived. And you can hardly expect me to bring her back in a day." He opened his palms toward Stefano. "Music is not giving her any joy. She hungers only for more of the fame she has tasted once. I've known fame; I've walked this path. Have you?"

Again, Stefano stood silenced. Donizetti felt the pull from his tomb strengthening still; he fought not to stagger visibly backward. He spoke faster.

"Because if you can heal her, then yes, please, send me back to my rest. But if you can't ... then for the rest of your life, you can look back on this as the night that you, and you alone, chose to consign her best hope to the grave."

Stefano's fist tightened on the crucifix, until Donizetti thought the wood might snap in his hand. Then, of a sudden, he lowered it to his side. He stepped closer to the circle of candles, to within a few centimeters of Donizetti's shimmering face. "You had better be right. About what she needs."

He turned to the priest. "Thank you, Padre. And sorry to have troubled you." The priest lowered his own crucifix and slumped with relief. Stefano extinguished one of the candles beneath his shoe.

Donizetti stepped over the dark candle, out of the circle.

"Thank you for trusting me," he told Stefano.

"Who said I trusted you? I'm a desperate man."

Donizetti nodded and said, "It should not be much longer." Then he vanished.

That night, when Simona met Stefano at the concert, he smiled cautiously and gave her a slow nod that was almost a formal bow. He said nothing in greeting, likely for fear of saying the wrong thing. It felt to Simona like the first meeting of ambassadors after the conclusion of a war.

They took their seats. Stefano, to break the tension, read an anecdote about Verdi from the program. "Have you heard this story before?" he asked. "While writing *Il Trovatore*, Verdi received a visit from a noted critic. He played three tunes from his work in progress, and the critic informed him that they were all absolute, irredeemable trash. 'My friend,' Verdi enthused, 'thank you! This is to be a *popular* opera. If you had liked it, no one else would. But your distaste promises me great success!'"

It was a hopelessly awkward attempt at safe conversation, reading from the program instead of sharing their own thoughts. But it was also a relief, so Simona went along with it.

"I've never heard that," she admitted. "But then, *Il Trovatore* is what, his twelfth opera?"

"It says here his eighteenth."

"Well, then. I hope by the time I've written eighteen operas, I'll have the stature to tell the critics how useless they are, too."

"If I know you, I think you'll prefer their approval, even then."

She smiled, a little ruefully. "You do know me."

She held his hand while the music played, adjusting her grip constantly.

Tighter to reassure him, then looser because her palm felt too clammy to inflict on him.

She felt Stefano lose himself in the music when it started. He did not compose, and played with only a hobbyist's skill, but he was a knowledgeable, appreciative listener. Beside her, he closed his eyes. His head drifted from side to side with each swell of the music, like a conductor's baton in slow motion.

Images of written music tumbled through Simona's mind as the orchestra played. For brief stretches, she could stop herself compulsively rewriting the music as it entered her ears. But soon, the concert became just another exercise in composition. She could improve upon the music for a few measures at a time, then her rewrites would dissolve into cacophony—while the original continued to fill the theater with its infuriating flawlessness.

"I'm sorry I sent you away so abruptly the other night," she told Stefano at the intermission. "My work has me on edge, but I never meant to make you doubt our relationship."

"No, I'm sorry," he said. "For trying to protect you from yourself. You were right. Your gift for music is part of what I love in you. I have no business telling you how to write it."

You love me for my music, she thought, *but what if my music is gone?* That thought would not reassure him. So she wrapped her arms around him and said nothing.

They returned to their seats. The second half of the concert proved more trying for Simona than the first. She listened with a feverish intensity, gripping her armrest with white-knuckled force. She listened as if lives were at stake.

She wanted to be uplifted by the music, enlightened, transformed. She wanted the sounds of instruments and voices to part like a curtain, to reveal some large and glorious truth. She wanted a dormant part of herself to awaken, to resonate with Verdi's music and answer it in a voice of her own.

The music was lively and lovely, but she wanted it to be more than it was. It blithely refused, and she felt sick. Betrayed—though whether by Verdi or by herself, she could not be sure.

Am I learning to hate music? Is that what's happening to me?

At the end of the night, Simona had no auditory memory of the concert. She recalled only the gleam of brass, the black of formal wear, the dancing baton.

The next morning, a Saturday, Simona called her friend Donna. She apologized for missing her party and made plans to meet her that afternoon for a belated birthday lunch. Then she went out to find Donizetti and tell him she would not be continuing her studies. She would not frame it as an admission of failure. It would be an admission that the joy had gone out of trying.

She could not find him in his museum, though. Nor was he at Santa Maria Maggiore. Could he have anticipated her decision to abandon the composing life?

She looked for him in each of the places they had haunted: the bell tower, La Rocca, the café on the Piazza Vecchia. She did not expect to find him, but she felt a duty to be thorough.

When she saw the billowing flag at La Rocca, she heard music in her mind, very faintly. She caught herself humming along with it, and made herself stop.

She drifted through the city, meandering toward the path that ran along the inside of the city wall. The sun shone in a clear sky, and a warm breeze carried the scent of autumn through the streets.

What will I do in the next phase of my life? There was optimism in the question, she was surprised to discover.

She wondered again about Donizetti. Had she disappointed him, or had he meant for her journey to lead here? She stopped at the point on the city wall where they had talked before, and tried to imagine seeing *Città Bassa* through his eyes, watching his descendants' headlong rush toward the future.

She sensed him at her side before he spoke.

"Two hundred years ago, that was a field of trees," said Donizetti. "They were just beginning to build houses down there. How do I feel about your automobiles, your Internet?" He shrugged. "How would my ancestors have felt about my pocket watch, when the clock on the bell tower was once the only timepiece in the city? Who were they to judge, and who am I? People are still people, and that is all I ever was."

He turned to face her. "If I may presume to speak for the long-dead, I thank you for preserving our old, familiar home in a position of honor." He looked out over the wall again, and so did she. "But thank you also for continuing to build. I am pleased to see that Bergamo still lives and breathes."

Simona smiled. She turned to look at Donizetti, to thank him for the time he had spent with her—even to kiss him, if his cheek had enough solidity to receive the gesture—but he had vanished.

She had never actually said the words to let him know that their study sessions were at an end. Somehow, he had seemed to know it already.

If he had, in some oblique way, replied to that knowledge, it was without the disappointment she might have expected.

She lingered by the wall for a moment, overlooking the modern city that was now her home, beneath the stately city that had once been all of Bergamo. Then she set out walking. It was nearly time for her lunch with Donna.

The birds that nested in the trees beneath the wall were singing. Simona whistled a few notes back to them, first mimicking, then harmonizing. Until recently, she would have felt an anxious impulse to remember those notes for later, in case they might be the seeds of her next great work. Now that impulse was gone. The birdsong existed in that one beautiful moment—and when the moment passed, it simply passed.

She was still whistling to herself when she approached the restaurant. Donna had secured an outdoor table for them and was waiting. She stood up to greet Simona, smiling.

"You sound like a bird."

Simona looked confused for a moment, then realization dawned, and she laughed. She hadn't noticed herself whistling. "I must have been imitating them."

Simona apologized again for missing the party, but Donna waved it off. "Like I said on the phone, I'm glad you were just doing your tortured artist thing, and not sick or injured."

It was the same restaurant where Donizetti had taken her, just prior to her breakdown. Simona ordered a small pizza, knowing that this time, she would be permitted to eat the whole thing, instead of trying to compose it.

She and Donna had known each other since childhood, and could talk to each other about anything. So when Donna asked her how the 'tortured artist thing' was going, Simona decided to tell her the whole story. It wouldn't have felt right talking to Stefano about Donizetti's ghost; it would only have made him worry. But Donna, after a few moments of understandable disbelief, reacted with simple wonder—and most of all, with interest in the relationship Simona had formed with her celebrated mentor.

"So, let's pretend I believe you," Donna said, "that you could really give up composing for more than a month or two."

"You're so accommodating!"

"Purely for the sake of argument. Have you thought about what kind of work you'll do instead?"

Simona pursed her lips. "I might teach children to play," she ventured. "I know the violin, cello, and the piano well enough to teach them."

Donna nodded encouragingly. "That's good!"

"Maybe write the occasional advertising jingle. Score a few episodes of TV, if I can find out who I need to know."

Donna let a wicked gleam come into her eye. "So you're giving up music to work with ... music?"

Simona grinned sheepishly down at the table. "Well, that's hardly *real* composing, you know? It's more ... are you a chef going for that next Michelin star? Or are you just grilling a quick dinner on your terrace?"

The waitress arrived and set a plate in front of each of them.

Donna sipped at her drink. Simona expected her to continue asking questions about her music, and her identity as a musician—questions for which Simona didn't have coherent answers yet. But Donna must have sensed that it was a tender topic, so instead, she launched into a bit of gossip about her birthday party. Two of their mutual friends had arrived separately, but left together.

"Oh, they're all wrong for each other!" Simona exclaimed with delighted horror.

"Completely," Donna agreed. "But I don't think they'll realize it for a while, so I'm happy for them. It will be a beautiful mistake."

Simona glanced upward. She could see a jet rising into the sky, leaving a thin trail of white across the clear blue. It passed behind the dome of the basilica and continued on its way—a modern marvel slicing across the medieval skyline.

"A beautiful mistake," she echoed. "I have to say, that would be a *great* title for a piece of music!"

Donna raised an eyebrow as innocently as she could. "Really?"

"Oh, sure," Simona enthused. "You could have the lovers who seem all wrong for each other ... only in the end, of course, they aren't. Total opposites: one sings high and lively, with a lot of suspended chords. The other sings low and slow, and everything resolves neatly."

"So interesting."

"And the 'beautiful mistake' motif wouldn't only appear in their relationship. You could work it into other parts of their lives, into the set design, the architecture. The costumes."

Donna was biting down on her lip, and Simona abruptly realized she was doing it to prevent herself from bursting out laughing.

Simona leaned back in her chair, shaking her head slightly. "I guess *that* habit isn't going to disappear overnight."

Donna grinned broadly. "Clearly not."

"Sorry."

"You're apologizing to me?"

"You have to understand," Simona said, "I'm not latching onto this idea because I think it's magically going to wash away all of my troubles and turn me into a great composer again. I'm just ..."

"Being playful," Donna supplied. "Over lunch."

"Exactly."

If Donna realized that it wasn't quite the first time Simona had playfully talked over a musical idea during one of their meals together, then at least neither of them felt compelled to comment on the last time it had happened, nor on how very far that idea had gone.

"Exactly," Donna echoed.

Simona took a bite of her pizza—and as the flavors burst across her tongue, the world seemed to slow, so she could linger in their perfection. She made a soft noise of pleasure. Her features melted into a serene smile, and her eyes closed.

Donna watched her head sway slowly as if she were dancing, while, in her mouth, the flavors sang.

See Charles Schoenfeld's story "The Preserved City" online at Metaphorosis.
If you liked it, leave a comment. Authors love that!
Remember to subscribe to our e-mail updates so you'll know when new stories are posted.

About the story

I used to work for the American branch of a company that had its global headquarters in Bergamo, Italy. Once, my job sent me to Bergamo for a week. I spent the daytime in an office, but in the evenings and on the weekend, I was free to explore the town. With the exception of Simona's apartment, I visited each of the settings that later found their way into the story.

Either during that trip or shortly afterward, a single image came into my mind, and I knew I wanted to write a story around that image. I pictured two ghosts from Bergamo's medieval past, standing by the city wall, looking out across the valley, across the modern portion of the city that had not yet existed in their own time, and having a conversation. I pictured them from the perspective of a modern person somewhere beneath the wall, looking upward, seeing the moon shine faintly through one of their translucent heads and realizing that they were ghosts. This living observer would naturally wonder what they were talking about. What did they think of the modern way of life? Were they proud, amazed, disappointed?

That exact image didn't find its way into the finished story, though an echo of it did. Instead of two ghosts, it was a ghost and a living person. And the living person had a problem for which the city's dual nature —past and present, side by side—served as a metaphor. I wrote the first draft of the story during the six-week Clarion writing workshop. It was my second story of the workshop, so maybe subconsciously I was feeling some of the same pressure as my protagonist, to make sure my second offering was at least as good as my first one.

A question for the author

Q: What's your writing schedule?

A: I'm about as far removed from a morning person as it's possible to be. My body would prefer to keep vampire hours, if my day job didn't require otherwise. So I do most of my writing late into the night, and on weekends.

About the author

Charles Schoenfeld is a graduate of the Clarion science fiction & fantasy writers' workshop, and a past finalist in the L. Ron Hubbard Writers of the Future Contest. He has worked with more than a dozen community theatres in New England, as a leading actor, playwright, director, and fight choreographer. Charles lives in Connecticut with his daughter, Leila, and devotes much of his energy to the pursuit of chocolate cake.

A Death in New York

Allison Brice

There are decisions that we know immediately are good. There are decisions that we know immediately are bad. There are decisions that we know immediately are horrific, atrocious, I'll-regret-this-for-the-rest-of-my-life bad.

I specialized in the third category.

"Glad to see you still haven't gotten rid of that broken lampshade," Tyler said, reaching behind her to take her bra off.

"Fuck you," I said with a bite to her lower lip, slapping her hands out of the way so that I could unhook it with one hand. Tyler shivered, even though that particular lesbian trick had never impressed her before.

I nudged her into bed, next to the lamp with, yes, a very broken lampshade, and we went down hard into my twisted-up, unwashed bedsheets. I wanted to be embarrassed about the way I hadn't changed since we'd been together, about the way that I'd taken our beautiful, open, airy room and turned it into my dark, weird cave with mandala tapestries and overflowing ashtrays. And I *was* embarrassed, at least a little. Mostly I was horny.

"Jesus, Soph, *ow*, with the biting," she said, as I sucked a desperate hickey into the inside of her thigh. "That's gonna bruise."

Good, I thought viciously. If she saw a mark from me for the next week, then I wouldn't be forgotten. She'd have to think about me, at least for a little bit, think about me and the life she left behind and the Upper East Side apartment she left in my name with no thought at all to how expensive that was.

I took the hair tie off my wrist and pulled my hair into a sloppy bun. Tyler lounged back on the bed with her hands already fisted into what little blonde hair she had. I ducked down, spread her knees apart, belly-flopped forward until I was pressed up against her musky darkness. I had been celibate for far too long, and yes, Tyler was about the worst person I could have slept with, but I'd seen her at Trader Joe's and she always had a beautiful smile and I gave a first, tentative lick —

"Sophie."

Nope, I thought, with my nose pressed right to the core of her. *No, not tonight.*

"Sophie."

"Go away," I said, muffled. Tyler snorted a laugh.

"The disposal is broken. Come fix it."

"New roomie struggles?" Tyler said, with a terrible grin.

"You have — very literally — no idea," I said. To the thing standing outside the door, I said, "We can fix it tomorrow. If you put string cheese wrappers down the sink, then the disposal breaks."

"Sophie, I want to fix it now. Stop playing with the weird girl."

"Go *away*."

I smiled sheepishly at Tyler (and God was I sick of apologizing to this girl), put a hand on her knee and kissed the join of her hip and thigh.

Then I heard the jiggle of the door handle. "Sophie —"

"Shit!" I grabbed the blankets and threw them over Tyler. "Do *not* come inside, I mean it!"

Tyler rolled her eyes, grabbed her phone to flick through it. Blushing, furious, I stuffed myself into a gigantic t-shirt and opened the door, face-to-face with the new roommate I'd been stuck with since Tyler left me.

"We talked about this," I said to Death. "When my door is closed you leave me alone."

Death blinked their massive grey eyes. "But the disposal."

"Fuck the disposal, I'll fix it tomorrow. Aren't you supposed to be out shepherding lost souls? Isn't there anywhere else you could be that's not cockblocking me?"

"The minions are working tonight," they replied. "I wanted to listen to One Direction but now the disposal is broken and I can't listen to music when the disposal is broken."

"That doesn't make any sense! Just go in your room —"

"Sophie," they said, pathetic with their limp hair and Avenged Sevenfold t-shirt and big, sad eyes. "I nccd you to fix the disposal."

They would stand here all night. Death would stand outside my door until I fixed the disposal. And if that wasn't the worst boner-killer I'd ever heard.

I sighed and went back inside my room. I couldn't make eye contact with Tyler when I said, "Maybe it's best if you come back another night."

She wouldn't come back another night. This had been my one chance and we both knew it. She gave a weird little smirk and rolled over to grab her shirt.

"Seems like you lowered your standards," she said meanly.

It's funny that she thought I had standards.

This may sound hard to believe, but interrupting my non-existent sex life was not the only problem that came with having Death as a roommate. It was, however, the final impetus for a raging fight.

"And you never take out the trash!" I screamed.

"And you don't let me play my music over the speakers," Death replied, never raising their voice.

"That's because I'm not listening to One Direction *again!* Your taste in music is shit!" I would feel bad that the neighbors could hear us, but we lived in Manhattan. Our walls were so thin I could tell whether George and Amber in number 4 were having missionary or doggystyle.

"If you would just let me get a cat —"

"Oh no, not this again," I said. It didn't help that Death had picked a particularly pathetic human suit today. Instead of their usual borderline-pedophile man, today it was a small, perky, blonde woman. I felt like I was screaming at Kristin Chenoweth. "We're not getting a cat. I would end up doing all the work and taking out the cat shit and you would get all the snuggles. Absolutely not."

"Sophie," they said. Big, sad, blue eyes. Looking just like all the girls that used to call me weird in middle school. "Please. I want a cat."

"Kiss my ass," I replied.

When I was unmoving, Death finally spoke. "Our Father, who art in Heaven —"

"Oh, shit, don't do that —"

"Hallowed be thy name —"

"No, anyone but her —"

"Thy kingdom come, thy will —"

"I'm here," God said. She appeared, like she always did, out of thin air, and the walls of the apartment bulged with the power of two immortal beings. Unlike Death, who took pleasure in switching up their appearance and gender, God was the same every time I saw her: a chubby, harried middle-aged woman with brown hair. She typed furiously into an iPhone and didn't look up at us. "Hello, Death. Hello, Sophie. This had better be important."

"I can't do this anymore," I said immediately. "Death is the absolute worst. I want out of the contract."

"You want out of the contract?" She said, looking up over her phone. "You want out of free rent, paid-off student loans, a raise at work, and a miraculous cure for your step-grandmother's pancreatic cancer?"

That gave me pause. Just as it had the first time she'd offered it.

"Let her go," Death said flatly. "She's terrible. She didn't fix the disposal and she wouldn't come out to help me because she was having bad sex."

"Do you know how long it's been since I got laid?" I spat. "I was *this close* to finally having a good orgasm before your useless ass —"

"This is not productive," God said. "Obviously you haven't bonded. In order to make this arrangement work, you have to be able to understand each other."

"Let me out of this stupid arrangement," Death said, a rare note of bass in their voice. But God didn't even blink.

"No. Your bedside manner is atrocious and you have lost all touch with humanity. We agreed, Death, living with a human is going to be good for you. Now," she said, as Death and I both opened our mouths to argue, "you two have to spend more time together. I want to see you having a productive conversation about how you're going to make this arrangement work. Sometime in the next few days will work just fine. Now, if you'll excuse me."

And just like that she was gone. The apartment felt normal again — tiny and overpriced, yes, but slightly normal. Except for the immortal being sitting on my sofa, pouting their big pink lips.

"I'm going to Trader Joe's," I said to Death.

The apartment always smelled vaguely musty. Even back when it was me and Tyler living here, there was something off about the walls. Mold, maybe. Asbestos. It's New York, it could be anything.

Death did not improve the situation.

"You need a shower," I said, upon coming home with a twelve-pack of White Claw. If I was going to bond with Death, there was no way I was going to do it sober.

"I showered this morning." They sat on the couch, mindlessly flicking through Netflix. They were in a new male body today — a very attractive one, I might add, Black and trim and gorgeous. I'm gay, but I have eyes.

"Did you actually turn the water on or did you just stand in the shower and touch the tiles?"

Death looked at me plaintively. "They are very soothing to the touch."

"Oh my God." I pulled one out of the cans, cracked it open and drank it warm.

"What are you drinking? I thought animal claws were not to be eaten?" they asked.

I looked down at the can in my hand. "What? It's not actually — it's White Claw. It's hard seltzer." Death looked at me blankly. "It's carbonated water, but with alcohol in it. I didn't want to love it, but it's delicious. Have you never had White Claw?"

They shook their head.

I pulled another one out of the pack and tossed it over. They caught it clumsily, like a six-year-old at a t-ball game. "Here you go. Nectar of the gods."

"This substance is ambrosia?" They sniffed it and then tried to lick the top of the can. I snorted.

"No, you just – you drink it, like a normal human. Pull the tab, put your lips to it and swallow."

Slowly, painstakingly, they cracked the tab with unnaturally long fingernails. Then they finally lifted it up and drank it, and then before my eyes Death drained the entire can in one swallow.

"I guess you liked it?" I said, biting down a chuckle.

Death shrugged. "It's fine."

"That's what we all say. Wait until the third one hits you. Let me get you some more."

I wasn't passing up a chance to get drunk with Death, that's all I'm saying.

An hour later we'd cleaned out all the seltzer I owned and had moved on to more intellectual topics. "So every week he picks the girls he likes and then he sends the rest of them home?" Death said slowly.

"Yes, exactly. The ones he likes gets a rose and then the ones he doesn't go home."

"But how much time has he actually spent with them? The ones who receive the rose?"

"Not much. Maybe an hour or so, if they're lucky?"

"And 'the Bachelor' is meant to make a decision about his future wife from this? How does he know if she is in it for the right reasons?"

"Exactly!" I said, drunkenly staggering upright and slapping the couch cushions. "You never know if they're in it for the right reasons! Who's here for love and who's just here for Instagram followers?"

"Is that why you have never gone on this show?" Death asked. Without my noticing it, we each had a can of seltzer in our hands, even though I was positive we'd finished them all. Finally using those superpowers for good.

I laughed, though it sounded like a cackle. "Uh, no. I haven't gone on the Bachelor because I'm not pretty enough and not straight enough."

"Ah, so the show does not allow lesbians. I see."

"Wait, does being gay actually send me to Hell?" I asked.

"No," Death said, sending a tidal wave of relief through my body. Apparently I'd been more concerned about that than I thought. So much for my liberal laissez-faire. "You will not go to 'Hell' for being gay."

The way they said 'Hell' made me very curious, but I knew they wouldn't tell me anything about the afterlife. I'd already tried asking, the first week we lived together, and been promptly shut down. I switched tactics. "What's your sexuality? Do you date? Have you ever been in a relationship?"

Death paused and thought about it. Their fingernails curled across the seltzer can. "God and I have been together since time immemorial."

"No, you can't date God. She doesn't count. Nobody else who you had a special connection to?"

"No."

Death's voice didn't give anything away, no emotional inflection at all. Still, my heart ached for them, just a little. Their life sounded lonely. "Okay. That's okay. Well, I, uh. I hope you find someone. I hope you feel that. Because it's wonderful, to feel like you've found your person. And it's the person who you want to talk to about everything, and maybe you didn't make any promises to be together forever, but...you assumed that they wouldn't want to go anywhere 'cause they always seemed so happy." I caught myself, because this was one spiral I didn't want to travel down. "Anyway. Being in love is awesome. But it's also kinda exhausting. I know I should date more, but...it's hard, sometimes. To move on."

"Where is your ex-girlfriend now?"

"Tyler? She's probably at her best friend's for board game night right now. She lives four blocks down; we go to the same Trader Joe's."

"Tyler...that is a boy's name?"

"Names don't have a gender," I said immediately, parroting the phrase I'd heard every day for all three years of our relationship, and then stopped myself. "But. Yeah."

"And you are not invited to board game night? Why not? You two had sexual relations."

"That was a bad idea, I shouldn't have done that. And I'm not invited to board game night because those are her friends, not mine. Every couple has groups of friends that they bring into a relationship, and then they keep their friends after they breakup. Except I didn't bring any friends, really, 'cause I moved here from Columbus for Tyler, so..." The room spun and swung around me; I was officially drunk with Death, and talking about Tyler of all people. How fucking pathetic. I hiccuped and swallowed down a wave of vomit. "I don't, like. Have a lot of friends."

Death blinked. "And you find this isolating?"

I nodded. "Yeah." My eyes watered, suddenly, pathetically. "I do."

"Do you wish to move back to Columbus?"

"I don't know. Maybe. There's nothing for me there. I wasn't any happier there.

I'd go just for my grandma, but she's pretty old and one time she told me that there wasn't any point in a young person wasting their life on someone who was going to die soon anyway." It occurred to me how strange this was, to be voicing this to Death, but they didn't react. Of course they didn't, of course they didn't react to themselves. "But I don't really want to stay here either, so I just don't know. I don't want to start from scratch all over again, I like my job but that's about it..."

"You need to discover what you want to do in life," Death said calmly. "You lack purpose and direction. You are adrift. You must decide what to do with the time you are given."

"Yeah, I get it, can we stop talking about this?" I snapped, alcohol slurring my words. "Can we talk about anything else? Damn."

Death actually leaned back a little, startled. To my drunken mind, that didn't make a lot of sense — weren't people always angry at Death? Surely I wasn't the angriest person to ever confront them? I felt bad, suddenly, for getting upset; that I was another human in a long line to be pissed at Death for doing their job. I shifted my anger.

"Why doesn't God help me find my purpose?" I said sarcastically. "Should I pray and see if she can come down and help me figure out what I'm doing in New York?"

"She wouldn't answer," Death said. "She never really helps you."

Their voice was bitter, laced with arsenic. I looked over to see Death moodily sipping their White Claw.

"That's a lot of emotions," I said. "Wanna talk about it?"

Death said nothing. The neighbors started arguing again; with our paper-thin walls, we could hear every shout. George had decided to spend more money on lotto tickets again, when Amber said that there were better ways to spend the money that *she* earned. It was a familiar refrain. Made me want to talk softly so they didn't hear the wacky shit in apartment 3.

"God looks out for my best interest," they said. "But I do not need her to. I have existed as long as she has. Her maternal efforts are useless and infantilizing."

Oh, this was good. "Like what?"

"Like you," they said immediately. "Moving into this apartment, ostensibly to relearn my 'bedside manner'. She says I have forgotten how to talk to humans. I ask her, am I meant to be smiling when I am never greeted with a smile? She has no idea what I do, the unceasing burden of my existence, and she saddles me with this apartment and this human form in order to make herself feel better."

In all our months living together I'd never heard them sound like that. "Sitting around with you does nothing to make my existence less agonizing. Knowing the name of this drink does not mean that the next person whose loved one I take will be less angry. This is a performative, empty gesture, and she knows it."

"So why do it?" I asked. "Why go along with it when you knew it was stupid?"

Death took another sip of White Claw. It was a very human gesture of delay. "I don't know," they replied. "Only that... what was the point of arguing? Why delay the inevitable? She always gets what she wants, in the end. I went along with it. I always go along with it."

In the next apartment, George and Amber had stopped arguing. I lowered my voice so they wouldn't hear my next sentence. "Can you, like, stick it to her? Fuck the police? I got arrested a lot in college for protesting, I can help you out." I got arrested more often for trespassing than protesting, but no need to throw myself under the bus.

"One does not stick it to God," Death replied, with a hint of amusement. "She could even kill people, do my job for me, if she wanted to. But she says she's not 'as good at it' as I am, and I must assume that I exist to end joy, just as she exists to bring joy. Obviously this makes her much more popular than I am. And if I do what I am told, I get to fly under her radar, and she does not bother me. I get to live a quiet existence."

"Baby," I said, cracking another White Claw, "that's the strategy I've been using for 27 years."

Baths are my preferred form of self-care. I understand that 'self-care' means more than just spending excessive amounts of money on bougie bath salts; people who really practice self-care go to bed on time, take care of their skin, work out and probably contribute productively to society. But nobody likes those people. So I take baths.

I stretched out and wiggled my toes against the grout, which desperately needed a scrub. Do you know how rare it is to find a Manhattan apartment with a full-size bathtub? There was a reason I'd put up with Death's nonsense in order to keep this place.

The other reason made my phone ring in my room.

I sat up immediately, sloshing water over the side of the tub. That particular harp ringtone was reserved for my grandmother. My very sick, very old grandmother.

"Death!" I screamed, hoping it would make it to the living room. "I need you to get my phone!"

"What?" they said.

"My *phone*, can you get it?"

I could have called her back, I know. But I was perpetually terrified that this was the call, the one that would tell me that my grandmother died, despite the fact that I'd literally bargained with God to ensure that wouldn't happen. My grandma is the most important person in my life. She's my step-grandma, technically, but of all the step- and half-siblings that I got during the divorce, collected and dropped like trading cards, she was the only one who stuck around. When I was branded as the difficult one in high school, when the rest of them decided that there wasn't enough behind my vitriol to get to know, she stayed, and talked to me, and slowly wore me down. We baked fucking cookies together, and we weren't even related by blood. When she got cancer, I thought, *Here goes the last person on Earth who'll ever care about me.*

All of this drama with God and Death was worth it for her. I clumsily got out of the bathtub, soap suds still in my hair, and lunged for the towel. I heard Death's plodding footsteps across the apartment, and suddenly I was utterly terrified of what I'd asked them to do.

"Yes?" Death said into the phone. "Hello. No, Sophie is in the bathtub. This is her roommate." They paused. "My name is Tiffany." With a deep, masculine voice. I groaned and rubbed myself dry as quickly as I could.

"I am doing well today, thank you. The Bachelor last night made the right decision and that made me happy during the day today." Another pause. "Yes, Sophie and I watch it together. Yes, it is wonderful. No, I don't think Sarah really loved him. I quite agree. Something about her." Another pause. "If it's any consolation, she will not lead a happy life. Her ex-boyfriend —"

"Stop being omniscient on the phone with my grandma!" I whisper-yelled.

"Um. Do you like One Direction?"

I wrapped the towel under my armpits and finally managed to get into my room, where Death sat calmly on my bed, attempting to engage my grandmother about One Direction. They looked up at me through thick eyebrows and said, "Sophie is here and would like to speak to you." A pause. "It was…nice to talk to you too."

I couldn't help but smile at the bafflement in their voice. They handed me the phone and I mouthed, "Thank you." They nodded and shuffled out of the room.

"Hey, Grandma. How are you doing?"

"Wonderful! I *love* your new roommate. Seems so much nicer than that Tyler girl."

"Yeah, she is," I said, and wasn't even lying.

"Her voice was very deep, though. For a young lady."

"Uh. Yeah. It's a. It's a thyroid thing." I cleared my throat. "Tell me about bridge club!"

"Sophie, God is here."

"What?" I was just about to start masturbating. "Like, now?"

"Yes. Come to the living room."

I threw my head back on the pillow. Kids, don't make deals with the devil. You wind up with God in your living room and no time to enjoy the most basic pleasures in life.

I stomped out to the living room. Death sat lazily on the easy chair, in their standard white male loser body; God, as usual, was dressed in the best fashion that the outlet mall could buy.

"Hello, Sophie," she said, smiling widely. I grunted and sat down on the couch. "How is your day?"

"Fine. Very busy. Really don't have any time to chat."

"Well, I'll be out of your hair before long," she said, still with an unceasing customer service smile. "I just wanted to let you both know how thrilled I've been to see you getting along. Your deep conversations about life and love, Death helping out by meeting your grandmother...it's just wonderful to see!"

I looked over at Death to watch them roll their eyes. Like this wasn't the exact behavior we'd been complaining about. I winked back.

"I hope that this convinces you to trust me more readily in the future," God said, once again pulling out her iPhone. She'd been without it for two minutes; color me impressed. "I know that it's in vogue to rail against me, to claim that you know better and you have no need of my wisdom, but I often know what I'm doing. Just like with you and your ex, Sophie. I knew all along that was a terrible idea."

My stomach turned to ice. "What?"

"Oh, she was *awful* for you," God said, without even looking up from her phone. "Didn't ever actually love you. And I knew that the whole time, but I didn't say anything, to let you make that decision on your own. But maybe next time you'll come talk to me, let me in on your life, and you'll see what kind of guidance I can provide." I gaped at her while something built up inside me, roiling, whiting out my vision with rage.

"Alright, I'll leave you to it. You two have a great day!" She gave a jaunty little wave and vanished. The apartment went quiet, nothing but the ever-present noise of the A/C and the washing machine and the cars relentlessly zooming by outside.

I turned to Death, saw them wide-eyed and glued to their seat.

"That *bitch*," I said.

"And then she has the *gall*, the fucking *gall*, to stand there and say that she was doing it for *me!* For *my* best interest!" I yelled, letting my voice screech, making George and Amber quake next door.

"I know," Death said, from where they still sat in the easy chair, eyes watching my relentless pace around the living room. I'd worn a track in the carpet.

"It was not good for me, it was not my best interest, it was —" I paused, took a deep breath. "That relationship *broke* me. All the gaslighting, all the distance, all her coldness, the way that she just never cared about my career or what I wanted or even *me*...and God was okay with that? She was just *fine* letting me get torn up?"

"Yes," Death said. "She loves to say she knows best."

"Oh, does she? And really you're just doing what she wants. Like this apartment, right? She said it was my choice, when she first came to me she said I could choose, but really she knew what I would say. She knew how broke I was, she knew how Tyler left my name on the mortgage but I had no idea how to pay for it, and she saw this poor sucker and figured I was gonna be the perfect guinea pig for her little experiment."

"I'm sorry," Death said, still in that same flat tone of voice. "That she made you live with me."

I whirled around. "Hey, no. No. It's not you I'm mad at. I like living with you." The words struck me, how true they were, how I'd never thought them before. I doubled down. "I like living with you. It's her that I'm pissed at."

Death nodded, with a slight smile. And then the smile slipped off their face. "Sophie," they said, and a river of cold washed down my spine. "I have to kill Tyler."

"What?"

"It is her time. She has an undiagnosed heart condition. It will send her into cardiac arrest. The ambulance will be called but they will come too late because there is no defibrillator at her office. She will be pronounced dead at the scene. It will happen tomorrow at 2:09 in the afternoon."

"*What?* She's 29, why is she dying? And why are you telling me?"

"So that you can say goodbye," they said solemnly. "I tried to intervene with God, to get her a special dispensation, but God said no. So I, um. I got you White Claw. In case you are sad. To cheer you up."

I dropped onto the rickety couch, my head ringing like a bell. Tyler was going to *die*? Tyler, with her undercut and her aloofness, Tyler with her fifty different board games, her mother's only child? And I was supposed to walk over there and say goodbye without saying goodbye, invite myself into my ex's house and bring her wine because only I knew that it was her last night on Earth?

"Why would you tell me this?" I said, my voice cracking. "You bastard..."

Death looked genuinely sad, pained. Deep lines cut through their face. "I know. But it is a privilege that you have. To know. If I did not tell you, you would also be upset with me."

"Don't put this on me," I lashed out. "Don't say you're doing this for me. If you really cared about me you wouldn't kill her." I looked up, locked eyes. "So don't do it. Don't kill her."

"What?" Death said.

"Don't kill her." I stood up and stalked over. "Come on. You don't have to kill her. She's 29, she's never done anything wrong except be a bitch."

"I have to lead her to the beyond," Death said. "That is my purpose."

"Well, it's a shitty purpose! Don't you want to take a day off? Don't you want to stick it to the man? Don't you want to stick it to *God*?" Oh, that felt good; molten heat built up in my bones. "You're tired of following her orders. You're tired of her forcing you to do unnecessary shit for her entertainment. You said she has no idea of the unceasing burden of your existence. Isn't it time she found out?"

Death took a step backwards, into the wall, away from me, my voice, my eyes, my tall body and my broad shoulders, my elbows that jammed into faces during basketball. Like every other kid in middle school, they were afraid of me.

Death was afraid of me.

"Listen to me. She doesn't control you. You control yourself. For a million years you managed your own destiny. Do it again. Leave Tyler out of it."

I could feel what we were doing, the blasphemy of it, deep inside me. My teeth couldn't stop grinding together and there was a cold sweat under my arms, around the back of my neck. I knew it was the eye of God watching us and I didn't care.

"Take a stand," I whispered, and I could see that I'd won.

Death nodded.

Maybe you shouldn't have dumped me, I thought, to the ex whose life I'd just saved.

When I woke up the next day, I was untethered. I laid in bed in my room and felt all the limitless possibilities of New York and America and the world outside. I called out sick from work and convinced Death to play hooky with me. We went to the Met and made a scavenger hunt to find all the racy art (which is when I, Sophie Collins, had the honor of explaining to Death how lesbian sex works, because they had no idea). Of all things Death liked the Asian art section the best; they lingered for a long time in front of a black stone carving of the god Shiva as conqueror of death. They stroked the small, carved fingers over and over, like a compulsion, until the guard came and yelled at them for destroying the precious artwork and unceremoniously booted us out.

After that we got pizza from the good place on 5th Avenue before wandering around the city. Death smiled and looked happy as they ate a deformed Spongebob popsicle, and I was so nervous it felt like I was going to shake apart. A part of me wanted to make sure that Death was with me when 2:09 hit, that I knew that they would follow through with their pact. A part of me wanted to hide from God, to take the subway underground all the way to Long Island and as far as I could go so she couldn't see me. A part of me wanted to climb on top of the fountain in Central Park and scream about what we were doing.

And then it was the afternoon, and Death was engrossed in some historical plaque, and I looked down at my watch and it was 2:09 on the dot. I said nothing, smoked my cigarette while people steered clear of Death with their pedophile-long hair, and at 2:10 I released all the breath in my lungs.

"You didn't trust me?" Death said, looking right at me.

"No," I replied, and Death smiled.

In retrospect it makes sense that we were at St. Patrick's Cathedral when I got the call. Death gave me a flat look when I wanted to go in, and I grinned back and dragged them by the hand inside. St. Patrick's is Catholic nonsense and Grandma would have a lot to say about these people with their idols up all over the place and the gaudiness of the stained glass, but I liked the majesty of it, the way that the cathedral soared over and around me without any input from anyone else. I especially liked watching Death, the way that they seemed calmer. Their eyes roved all over the space; not rapidly like someone seeing it for the first time, but slowly, carefully. Like they were seeking out their favorite parts, old stained glass windows and marble carvings, seeing if anything was different.

"Been here before?" I asked.

"Many times," they replied.

My phone went off, buzzing up a storm, causing glares from Death and a couple of Asian tourists. I pulled it out of my backpack and saw my mom's name flashing. The hairs on my neck stood up. I did not regularly talk with my mother.

"Uh, gimme a sec," I said. I ducked around the corner, next to the huge white statue by the altar. "Hi, Mom."

"Hi Soph," she said, with a sniffle in her voice. "Oh, hun, I don't want to be the one to tell you this."

"Tell me what?" I said, looking frantically at my watch. 3:16. Way past time.

"The home just called. Grandma…she was taking a nap and just…fell asleep. Apparently it was peaceful…" Her throat cracked, and my stomach dropped. *No.* "She just…I'm so sorry, I know you loved her, you can come home and say goodbye —"

I hung up, because I could see the guilt trip coming; the plea, even in one of the worst moments of my life, to come back home and take care of my mother in her pain. But my pain was also real, so real that I dropped into a pew, my knees buckling under me.

Death walked up. "What happened?"

"You mean you don't know?"

Death frowned. "Know what?"

I gaped, searching their face for signs of lying, because Death said that they had no idea about my grandmother's death, and if they didn't know then that meant —

In front of me, on the other side of the pew, God appeared.

I stared at her, mouth open and eyes wide, looking and feeling like a fish. "What?"

For the first time ever, God did not have an iPhone in her hands. They were clasped in front of her, in front of her sensible Ann Taylor blazer. "I'm sorry about your grandmother, Sophie. But it had to be done."

"What did you do?" Death said, sitting down beside me. God's face was still, lifeless, like the statue behind her.

"The two of you thought that you would scheme to ensure that Tyler Astin did not die today, as she was scheduled to. You offended the natural order of life, merely out of misplaced affection for a woman who left you. This behavior is unacceptable. You cannot dictate the flow of the world by abusing your relationship with Death. I had to step in."

"But that's against the contract," I said, dragging the words up. "When I moved in with Death. You would cure my grandmother's cancer. You broke the contract."

"I did no such thing," God said. "I cured your grandmother's cancer, as promised. She died of natural causes."

"You can't do that," I whispered, trying to stand up for myself even when all I wanted to do was fold to my knees and cry.

"You have no idea what I can do," God said, and a couple of people walking around her froze at the power in her voice. One man, engrossed in his phone, looked up and swerved away from her at the last second. *He almost bumped into God*, I thought hysterically.

"Keep that in mind the next time that you decide to rebel," she said, pulling out her iPhone again. "I am your God, Sophie Collins. You will respect me, or I will take all you hold dear and turn it to ash."

And just like that, she was gone.

I was left staring at the place she used to be, at the giant white marble statue. It showed a man and a woman, the man kneeling on the floor, slumped into the woman's arms, her face radiating static, frozen pain.

"Sophie, I'm sorry," Death said quietly. The rustle of conversation in the church was achingly loud. "I never thought that she would use her power on your family."

Grandma and I would never bake cookies again. I knew there were other revelations that would come later, but right now, this was the one stuck in my mind like a skipped disc. Grandma and I would never bake cookies again. She was the only one who'd ever bothered to make cookies with me. She was the only reason I'd ever go back to Ohio.

My eyes looked at the statue without really looking. The church slid in and out of focus. Tears welled up in my eyes, blurring the statue even more. I blinked them away, and finally recognized what the statue was supposed to be.

"Is that Jesus?"

Death nodded. "That is Jesus after he was taken down from the cross, lying in the lap of his mother."

"So he's dead there?"

"Yes."

"You killed him?"

Death blinked. "What?"

"Did you kill Jesus, or did God do it?"

One lady next to us overheard this conversation and turned to look at us. I fixed her with a glare and she backed away at the sight of my red eyes and tearstained cheeks and snarling mouth.

"I did it," Death said, with a heavy voice. "God did not want to kill her son, even though she was the one who said it was necessary. So I did the dirty work."

I relaxed back into the pew, just for a minute. My sadness started to ebb away, resolution calcifying in its place. Warmth filled me up, took roost in the marrow of my bones.

I might have found a reason to stay in New York.

"Okay, so you can kill a god," I said, stronger now, gathering speed. "You've done it before. You can do it again."

"What?"

"We're going after God," I said, and nothing had ever sounded so right. "You and I. We're going to take her down."

Death stared at me. I smiled, showing my canines.

They smiled back. Far, far above us, in the giant church spire, the great bell tolled across New York City.

See Allison Brice's story "A Death in New York" online at Metaphorosis.
If you liked it, leave a comment. Authors love that!

Remember to subscribe to our e-mail updates so you'll know when new stories are posted.

About the story

As a broke millennial living in an expensive city, I have had my fair share of roommates — some awesome, some awful. I have often used the phrase 'roommate from hell', and I thought that perhaps that could be literal. Living with Death as a roommate would certainly present some challenges. Would they clean up? How are their social skills? What music do they listen to? (No, non-existent, One Direction.) Obviously this would drive any normal person insane, so Death's roommate had to be just as much of a hot mess as they were. This created the character of Sophie, a crass, aimless, dirtbag lesbian who chain smokes and does not have her life together. Sophie, coincidentally, was named after my girlfriend's roommate's cat, who only occasionally allows me to pet her. New York is the city of possibilities, so that became my setting. I spent a lot of time there myself as a broke college student, so I remember some of my favorite haunts. The only thing missing was a wild card, someone to propel the story forward. Since the story already featured Death, why not add God? And while I was at it, why not make God a woman — a soccer mom, at that? Once those pieces were in place, I just ran with it to see where the story would go. Obviously, the answer was 'straight to Hell'.

A question for the author

Q: Do you write things other than speculative fiction?

A: Absolutely! I love the challenge of writing creative nonfiction; you have to write yourself as a character, with all the harshness and objectivity with which authors view their characters. I also have branched out into non-genre fiction, though in general if it's not at least a little fantastical I'm not interested. Also, I write critically acclaimed bathroom stall graffiti that has been published in multiple different languages.

About the author

Allison Brice was born in the deserts of Tucson, Arizona, but currently resides in Washington, DC. In her day job, she attempts to teach people United States history and mostly fails; at night she writes whatever comes to mind. She has never met a cow she did not like.

@_allisonbrice_

Tower of Mud and Straw

Yaroslav Barsukov

III. The Tulips

This is part 3 of Yaroslav Barsukov's novella, *Tower of Mud and Straw*. Parts 1 and 2 ran in September and October 2020. What has gone before:

The 'tulips' are destroyed, and Brielle tells Shea they have three months before the tower crumbles. Shea starts drinking.

In an attempt to cheer him up, Lena, the duke's lover, takes him on a hunt. Something strange happens: the deer they chase disappears, but Shea discounts this as a drunken episode.

Lena and Shea sleep with each other. Shea confesses his actions have doomed the tower; Lena is happy the threat of the Mimic Tower no longer looms over the world and tells Shea she'll be leaving Owenbeg soon.

Aidan, a Dumian émigré whom Shea knows from his days at the court, arrives in the duchy. Together, they trick Patrick, who's been planning another attempt on Shea's life, and leave him stranded in Duma.

Aidan reveals he wishes to ally himself with Shea. Shea's 'exile' turns out to be a test: the queen is grooming a potential successor and wants to see how he would handle the local lords. However, with the tower's destruction imminent, Shea has failed his assignment.

1

In silence, as though overcome with modesty, the doctor hid his instruments and rolled them into a piece of black velvet. A brass syringe, a pristine-white probe-razor, a speculum oculi. Shea wanted to open his mouth, but his face was a rubber mask after all the morphine.

It was his sister who spoke out loud the question everybody in the room must've been thinking. "Will he become an idiot?"

And even before the doctor could answer, Mother broke into tears.

"Catherine, please," Father said, putting his hand—always sandpaper-rough, clay-rough—on Mother's shoulder.

Undaunted, Lena took a step forward. "Will he be the same?"

"Probably." The doctor drummed his fingers on the black roll. "He has a concussion, but nothing worse than that, it seems. Pupils are of equal size. It's a miracle, actually, given the tree's height. Of course, tomorrow we'll know more. He should rest—and give him water, but do not feed him or he may choke on his own vomit."

They filed out of the bedroom, Lena last, her face an oil painting rendered mysterious in the afternoon light.

The next time Shea opened his eyes, the curtains fluttered around a scattering of stars.

The door creaked, letting in blackness from the corridor and, with it, his sister carrying a tray that smelled of warmth and bakery.

"I think…" His head swam, but at least he was able to talk; that was good. "I think the doctor said not to give me food."

"Who cares?" She lowered the tray, then herself, on the bed next to him. "I bet you you won't choke. Anyone but my brother. Besides, Grandma made black truffle waffles."

"Smells great."

"Tastes, too. Here, open your mouth."

A few minutes passed in counterpoint to two twelve year-old jaws, chewing.

"I've been thinking," Lena said. "I've been thinking. You know what we'll do, you and I?"

"What?"

"Guess."

"Ask Grandma to make more waffles?"

"When we're old enough, I want a beautiful workshop," she said, and the wind breathed through the window, lifting, thread by thread, the shadow of her hair. "Chairs and tables like on those pictures from the capital. Maybe wardrobes, too."

"A carpenter princess."

Even in darkness, he could guess a hint of her smile. "Go on. Sneer all you want—I'm the one with the waffle tray." She paused, and he saw a reflection in her eyes—perhaps the moon, perhaps the starlight, perhaps the future. "I just don't want Ma to feel sad anymore when she buys new furniture. And I want it to be yours and mine, brother. I want that place to be yours and mine."

"This is not really a betrayal, is it?"

In the courtyard of the Owenbeg castle, a thin dash of white: a woman Shea didn't know, waiting—for something or someone.

He leaned against the window frame. "Sis, I need to talk to someone. I already know the answers *they'll* give me—Aidan, Brielle. So I'm going to pretend she…" He waved the bottom of an empty whiskey bottle at the woman. "…she is you. Tell me if what I want to do is forgivable."

His mind's eye spun figures under the golden lights, men and women coming together, coming apart.

"I want to be there. At the royal court, at the Red Hill. I've always wanted to. We both wished for things in our lives, haven't we? You understand. I had no idea my exile was a test, sis."

In his eight years at the Hill, had he ever seen anyone break the waltz? *Funny how, in dance, you take each step of your own volition*, Shea thought, *and yet all the while you're following a goal somebody set up for you.*

"Damn it, sis—I can be a successor to Daelyn, can you imagine that? If I only play my cards right, if I rescue the tower. If I revert what I did earlier. Listen, can we, can we do it in the following way—"

The woman turned and looked in his direction. He straightened—*had she heard him?*—and pulled lightly at the curtain.

"Let's do it like this," he whispered. "It's different, now that I'm here. I know the risks. I'll personally make sure everyone using the tulips is properly trained. There'll be no accidents, no chewed walls, no more blood. Can we do it, can we do it like this?"

Am I striking a deal with my own conscience?

A man strode into the courtyard below, ran up to the woman, and spun her around in his arms.

2

"I can get us new Drakiri devices." Shea turned to Brielle. "But I need you to promise you won't allow junior artisans to work unsupervised."

"I promise. I promise." She sat on the sofa, at the same place he'd found her two weeks ago with a half-finished bottle of wine. None of that old desperation remained, though, no mocking smile, no slouched posture. All straight shoulders now, straight back, full of hope. "What made you change your mind about them?"

Shea didn't answer, looking at Aidan—who, from the window, said, "You still haven't told us where you're planning to get the devices."

"Does it matter?"

"It matters to me."

From under the rosewood trapdoor, Shea almost answered. "From an abandoned workshop in Musk Valley."

"Musk Valley?" Aidan slid his gloved fingers between the curtains and peeked at something outside. "There's that city— what's its name?—Oakvale?"

"Oakville."

"How many devices are we talking?" Brielle asked.

"Thirty or thirty-five, I don't quite remember."

The black glove let go of the curtains. "Will this be enough?"

"Well, it's a fraction of what the duke has destroyed," she said, "but if we concentrate all of them at one place, at the top of the tower, I think we can create a sufficient upward pull that would stabilize the structure. I must do the calculations, of course."

"Wouldn't it be dangerous, putting all eggs so close to each other?" Aidan asked.

"Yes, but also easier to supervise. However, we'll still need to convince the duke."

"I have a few ideas there." Aidan shifted his eyes to Shea. "What's Oakville to you?"

"Am I under interrogation?"

"And what if you were?"

"In that case," Shea said, "I would choose not to cooperate."

"Listen, I'm trying to help," Aidan said. "We simply don't have the time. I'd like to understand if you're at risk of running into a Patrick Number Two in Oakvale."

"Why would there be a Patrick Number Two?"

"Because I feel there's more to it than you let on. This workshop, was it yours? Your family's? Why was it abandoned? Did something happen there?"

"What's Oakville to you, Shea?" echoed Brielle.

He studied them both.

"Oakville is home."

And that was all he told them.

Later, in another room in his quarters, he rolled across the sweaty sheets, the fat angel staring at him from the ceiling.

A hand touched his shoulder. "Thank you."

"For what?" he said, eyes on the painting.

"It was nice."

"This time it was different. You're different, Lena."

"Different how?"

"Gentler—no, wait, that's not it. Happier, I guess."

She rose on her elbow, making no effort to cover her chest.

"I am happy. I want to run out naked into the courtyard and laugh, laugh, laugh."

"Better not do that, though."

"I won't." She chuckled and traced his cheek with her fingertips. "I'll be fine now."

He turned to her. "I don't understand you. That book, from the settlement—it's just a legend. You can't seriously believe in the Mimic Tower."

How could he tell her? How could he tell her he was about to undo everything, to smash that happiness into pieces?

She paused, contemplating something. "Imagine living at the foot of a great volcano. You live there in a village, a town, a city—doesn't matter. It's all the world you know. And then, one day, you learn the volcano will erupt in five years. And all will be gone, the houses, the people, the trees, the brook where you used to swim as a kid."

"I would probably move somewhere else."

"You can't, that's the problem. The ash would cover the skies until the earth itself would grow cold."

"Then I would eat, drink, and make love as much as I can before the end comes."

"Trust me, you wouldn't. I've been living with that kind of knowledge for years, Shea. It breaks you. Makes you cry like a baby at sunset."

"But that's the point," he said. "It's not knowledge, Lena. It's some text and a couple of drawings. You don't even know if the copy you showed me stayed true to the original book."

"Do you remember what I've told you about my mother?"

"You said she was a famous landscape painter."

"She had a period, right after my father had died, when she couldn't paint—so she took on menial jobs to get us by. One of those jobs was restoration. She restored everything, from paintings to old books."

"So it was her." Shea studied her face, her black hair cascading unto the pillow. "She introduced you to that legend, didn't she?"

"The Mimic Tower is real, Shea. We've avoided an apocalypse by a hairsbreadth."

Something bitter rose in him and splashed in acid against the windpipe. "You're a child. A beautiful, proud, misguided child."

He immediately regretted his words, the clumsy attempt at hurting her. *You're trying to hurt yourself,* he thought, *you prick, for what you're planning to do.*

He opened his mouth to apologize—but she simply smiled at him, something maternal passing through her eyes.

"Have you ever entertained a thought," she said, "that the universe may be more complex than we're ready to admit?"

He remembered. There had been a day in his childhood, a last day of spring—he'd been seven, and his biology teacher strode into the classroom brandishing two daguerreotypes.

Here, kids, is an octopus—and what do you see now? Holding up a picture of an aquarium (and in it, something with more limbs than a living being was entitled to), switching the images with the practiced movement of a circus magician.

I see only rocks.

Look closely. This stone to the left, it's him. Mimicking his environment. Live matter is capable of wondrous things, kids.

Can rocks mimic life, too?

No. No, of course not.

But behind the classroom's window, the sunlight had filtered through the branches of an apple tree, a lattice which reminded Shea of the veins on the back of his grandmother's palms, and an idea had occurred to him then—vague and half-formed as it was in a seven year-old's head—which echoed what Lena had said just now: that maybe life carried more facets than even the scholars knew.

"It doesn't matter." Lena sat on the bed. "Everything's fine now. It'll be a while before anyone would attempt another construction on this scale."

How can I tell her? Do I have the right anymore to this intimacy?

He remembered thinking he was a cart on a track, with no option but to press forward—during his speech at the council chamber, when he'd told the duke to get rid of the Drakiri devices. Now he was retracing his own steps, following the pas in a golden dance.

"I want to leave Owenbeg," Lena said. "I want to travel the world, now that I have it. You could join me."

"Join you?"

"Yes. Why stay? You've said yourself the queen will blame the tower on you. Why wait for that? Let's run away together."

She studied him, eyes glowing, and the ballroom in his mind shook.

"It'll be wonderful, you'll see. We'll travel with a caravan to someplace near the ocean, live in a house at the beach, listen to gulls in the evening. Let's do it, Shea. Let's do it right now, let's run away tomorrow."

For a moment, the dance moves no longer made sense. He imagined breathing in the smell of her skin, looking at the stars through the strands of her hair. He saw her, in a light linen dress, ankle-deep in water. Sat with her, feet dangling, at the edge of a caravan's wagon, pine trees full of sunlight passing them by.

Then he glanced at the angel again, at the olive branch extended toward the hunter. *Paintings are a lie. They're frozen in time, but nothing can stand still, and all things are moving, drawn to some faraway goal.*

"I need to leave for a week," he said. "Let's talk again when I'm back."

3

He heard his sister before he saw her—or rather, he heard a crowd's rumble coming from the direction of Sun Plaza. He'd expected her in the morning, but something must've intervened. It was getting late. Squeezed between the roof tiles, the evening was a baked crust, the same gold and terracotta reflecting, Shea knew, off the grapes at home, at the vineyard.

He turned away from the street and dove back into the workshop's twilight. At this hour, the hall reminded him of a belly of some great ship, shadows accentuating all the wheels suspended under the ceiling and all the ropes stretched between them.

"Danny!"

The only man still working raised his head from a sand-yellow cabinet.

"She's coming. It's time."

Danny was a bit slow. Well-meaning, hard-working, but slow. A few seconds dragged by before he nodded, wiped his hands on his apron, and followed Shea outside.

The rumble: two streets away now, judging by the acoustics. One.

When a wooden cart rolled into the square and in front of the workshop, it pulled behind it a dozen onlookers: a flock of baby ducks in their mother's wake. Lena sat atop a pile of something big, dark, egg-shaped.

Beaming, she waved at Shea. "Look at this, brother!"

For a moment, for him, she became the girl with whom he used to play hide-and-seek at the vineyard, and he realized he was already smiling back. He took her hand and helped her to the ground.

"You're alone, sis?"

"So. Why?" She dusted her trousers.

"Show's over, guys," he said, picking out with his eyes the tallest person in the crowd, a woman in a linen coif. Then, to Lena, "I thought we've agreed you'd bring a Drakiri to help us."

"Are you afraid of a couple of flowers?"

"Flowers?"

People began to disperse—but slowly, like sleepwalkers.

"Tulips." Lena patted one of the dark things lying on the cart. "They *are* tulips, don't you find?"

"I'm not sure. Eggs, at most."

"Wait until they bloom."

"So you know how to operate them?"

"Of course," she said. "And anything I don't know, we can figure out together."

He paused, studying her, studying the devices. "Okay. Let's unload them, then. Danny, would you…"

"No need to." Lena turned and touched a valve on the tulip's surface.

With her other hand, she nudged a lever. Both motions appeared natural, light, as though she were weaving or playing a harp.

The dark egg hummed and rose into the air like a giant bumblebee, prompting a collective sigh from the people who still lingered in the square.

"And then you do... this." She reached around and slapped the hovering thing on the side, sending it gliding toward Shea. "Catch it, brother. Catch it, Danny! Catch it!"

Lena's laughter followed them as they ran—clumsily, in Danny's case—after the Drakiri device, headed for a back alley.

4

"It'll come," Shea said. "Two more hills, and we'll see it."

The place where the river meets the land, where the hillside scoops the sun's honey and the toy white boats ride the ripples.

He didn't know whom he was telling this—certainly not that calm silence which sat across the table from him.

Aidan fished a piece of meat from his plate, eyes on the airship's window. The black gloves stayed on even when he ate.

The dining lounge hosted one more passenger, an old lady with large, veiny hands. Although she held on to a fork, she didn't appear to be eating: each time Shea glanced at her, it was the same posture, same lowered head, as if she'd started the motion but didn't have the strength to finish it.

"Something seems to be bothering you," Aidan said. "May I ask what?"

His earlier words echoed in Shea's mind—'we must get rid of Patrick, I'm afraid'—as if Aidan had applied a knife to the sentence the way he'd been ready to apply it to Patrick's throat.

"Why are you asking?"

"Because we share a common goal, and I've no desire to see it compromised. And because I still know nothing about this workshop of yours."

Sunlit hills flowed below, trees at that distance turning into gilded fur.

"Musk Valley is my home," Shea said.

"Fine, don't talk." Aidan folded his napkin. "You seem intent on rejecting my help."

"What do you want me to say? Listen, when I convinced the duke to destroy the Drakiri devices, I believed in what I was saying. The stuff's dangerous. Heaven knows how many were maimed at the tower, perhaps even died—were there any deaths? Do you know?"

"I don't. Not that I care much, mind you."

The old lady twitched the way people twitch in their sleep. The fork clanked against her plate, and she finally started eating.

"What the hell am I even doing," Shea said, "bringing more devices to Owenbeg?"

"A chance at the crown means nothing to you, does it? Then consider this: if the tower doesn't get finished within the next two years, Duma will attempt an incursion."

Shea couldn't contain a hiss. "Come on, are you one of those idiots who believe Duma has the densest population of megalomaniacs in the world?"

"I don't *believe* anything." Aidan skewed his mouth, from the looks of it probing his teeth in search of a wayward piece of food. "I *know*. Duma is my motherland, I spent the first thirteen years of my life there; I know how they think, their opinion of other countries, of *you*."

"Well, it's not like we have a lot to do, so why don't you convince me that they're the furnace of the world's evil?"

"I'll tell you a story, Shea." Aidan slouched in his chair a bit, but one of the black gloves squeezed into a fist, crumpling the napkin. "It was my father who'd decided, single-handedly, that we needed to leave the country. He decided it when the crown prince, only fifteen then, only three years older than me, assumed command of the royal cavalry battalion.

"People went crazy. You know how it happens: everybody ecstatic, everybody talking of a new emerging leader. Father, he saw the writing on the wall. One morning at the end of summer I woke up and saw him through the window, in the sun, exchanging papers with a man I didn't recognize.

"They shook hands, and the man left. Father turned and walked, too. I couldn't see him past the window's edge, but I knew the front door would bang in a few seconds, and that moment was for me—I realize it sounds trite, but still—it was a loss of innocence. My sisters, Maria and Isabel..." He paused. "Maria and Isabel slept in another room. I remember a toy, a bear, perched on the table in mine.

"The door banged and he walked in, or rather, darted through the anteroom. I heard him say something to Mother in a loud voice—normally, he was all quiet in the mornings, afraid of disturbing our sleep.

"When I tiptoed over the ice-cold floor, into the living room, Mother was collecting things, some silly stuff—pictures from the walls, porcelain cats from the shelves. Father told her to stop, pack the clothes, and wake us up.

"The carriage already waited outside. Our cook flapped her apron at her face, and the stable-hand, Michael, ran after us, waving his hands. Michael had first put me on a horse and taught me to ride."

Aidan slid away his plate. "Past the city gates, I remember, Father relaxed. He even smiled at me. Isabel asked for her doll. That was when the bomb exploded."

He traced with his fingers a pattern on the table.

"Something hit me on the head, and I flew out through the carriage's door like a sack. I sat on the pavement, bawling, snot all over my face. My hearing was gone. And you know what the worst thing is? I don't even remember the corpses. I remember a wheel rolling past me, people running toward us, but not the corpses.

"Mother and Father survived—Isabel and Maria didn't. It was Michael who'd planted the bomb, of course. They'd found out Father wanted to leave the country, and they bribed our stable hand to blow us up."

"I'm sorry, Aidan," Shea said.

"You don't have to be. It was twenty-five years ago; I healed. Which brings me to another point…" He pinched the rim of his glove. "You're afraid that people at the tower will never learn to work with the Drakiri devices? Well, you can live with these things for your entire life."

In one motion, he pulled the glove off. The old lady at the neighboring table gasped, and her fork rang like a little bell.

Aidan's arm ended at the wrist; what came after branched off in metal and purple veins, glowed in sparks, roughly following the contours of a human hand—but only roughly. Knotted 'fingers' rolled in the air as though strumming a chord.

Carefully, Aidan put the glove back on and smiled at the old lady who sat there with huge, frozen eyes.

Shea exhaled. "Gosh. I never knew."

"Now you do. The bomb maimed me, and I had this thing fitted instead by a wandering Drakiri craftsman when I was twenty-one."

"You said you found out it was Michael who'd planted the bomb. What did you do to him?"

Aidan didn't say anything, but his smile sharpened while the eyes went to ice.

Isabel, Maria. Lena. Shea exhaled, struck by an analogy. *I could've been Aidan. If it were a* person *that had taken Lena from me, I quite possibly would've been him.*

And then they passed the next hill, and, sure enough, there were the ripples on water, and the white sails, and the valley's saddle onto which a palette knife had scrawled the contours of a city.

Somehow, the magic of it appeared dull; all he could think about was a boy looking at dead bodies, an image that held, in itself, a similar picture from his own past, like a Dumian stacking doll.

5

Upon entering the workshop, Shea ducked in a nick of time to avoid getting smashed against the wall by a gliding wardrobe.

"Sorry, brother!"

He scanned the room but couldn't understand where Lena's voice was coming from.

On the far side of the hall, Danny and another worker caught the wardrobe and stabilized it in the air. It hung there, spinning lazily, surreal in the purple light that oozed from the 'tulip' fastened to its back. Danny stared at it, mouth open. Other pieces of furniture floated across the workshop, too—a mahogany dining table, a padded sofa for four, an oak-and-leather chair: a scene from someone's dream.

"Grand, isn't it?" Lena descended to the floor, sitting with legs crossed atop a Drakiri device.

"This is dangerous, sis. You could fall."

"Why don't you give it a ride yourself?" She smiled, rose, and tapped the inky surface. "Come on."

"No thank you."

The moment the tulip had touched down, the purple light inside began to die.

"Look." She waved around the hall. "No more hauling things. No more accidents when something falls on someone. We can have twice as much space, we can get rid of all the workbenches—people will work on the furniture while it's suspended in the air. Hey, they can even work outside if they wish."

"Why didn't you wait for me, sis? I thought we wanted to try those things out together."

"I thought so, too." She thumped her fist playfully on his arm. "But today, you seemed more interested in that new maid—what's her name? Muriel? Did you take her out to the vineyards?"

Shea felt red rising to his cheeks. "No. Listen, I had a talk with that Drakiri, you know, the one who works in the town hall."

"Mmm?"

"He told me those things—tulips, eggs, whatever you call them—they're dangerous. So dangerous, in fact, that I asked him to come here and take a look at them, and he wouldn't even consider it."

"Brother."

"He said they're volatile and difficult to operate."

"There's a valve, and there's a lever. You saw how *I* operated them—did it seem difficult to you?"

"I saw *you* working with them, sis, yes. What about the others here?"

"I can turn the tulips on and off. Once they're in the air, you don't need to do anything else, just push them here and there. I can take care of everything."

"Perhaps," Shea said. "But what if you get sick? What if something happens at home, and you have to leave in the middle of the day?"

"Hopefully nothing happens at home."

"Yes, but what if...?"

"Then we'll deal with it when we get there. Oh, and by the way..." She turned and ran her fingers across the tulip's surface, now completely dark. "I've ordered another thirty devices from the Drakiri settlement in Owenbeg. They'll arrive in a few days."

"What? No! This is my workshop as well as yours, and I forbid it. Even those six..." He glanced at the people trying to get hold of the rotating mahogany table. "...they may've been a mistake."

Something sparkled in her eyes. "Let's make a bet."

"A bet?"

"A bet. Like we did when we were children. Give me till tomorrow evening, and I bet you I'll change your mind about the tulips."

Shea chuckled. "What do you...?"

She smiled dreamily. "I have an idea." Without warning, she stepped forward and squeezed him in an embrace.

"Everything will be beautiful. You'll see, brother."

6

The carriage took them from the port's breeze into Oakville's narrow, sand-colored streets.

In no particular order: sunlight-watered shadows under the house bridges; a barber on the corner catching the clouds with his mirror; a bigger dog chasing a smaller one; a woman, her hand on her hip, talking to a man with bald temples.

Inconceivable how something could carry the sugary-powder flavor of childhood and, at the same time, a much more bitter, corroding taste.

"I never wanted to return," he said.

Aidan didn't respond.

Sun Plaza. Memory lane zigzagged around striped market stands, past doors the color of green bottle-glass. Summer always managed to prolong its stay here: yellow leaves on the cherry trees seemed simply an extension of daylight.

The driver half-turned to them. "Where to now?"

"Ashcr..." *Damn it.* Something made him swallow the word—whether it was the sun that stung his eyes, or all the things rising up his chest. "Ashcroft family workshop."

"What's that?"

"The furniture shop a few streets away."

"Oh." The man pursed his lips. "Oh. You mean Imogen's."

"I mean that street, right ahead. I'll show you the way from there."

What had he expected? After a decade —dead windows, still criss-crossed by wooden boards? Of course the place had a new owner, and he could only hope they hadn't discovered the rosewood trapdoor.

"You've mentioned the proprietor's name," he said.

"A gal called Imogen." The driver smacked his lips. "That shop, after what had happened, folks were afraid it was cursed or something. All those people who died—"

"What *did* happen there?" Aidan said.

The man shrugged. "People died. You know. Anyway, no one wanted to buy the place until Imogen came along and made it into a clothing store."

The carriage drove into a small square in front of a building which still reminded Shea—even though his young, romantic self had long faded—of a yacht: the dark wood of the first floor and the white sail of the second.

The sign read 'Flying Tulip Dresses.' Imogen hadn't simply bought the workshop—she'd bought its history, too.

Leaving the black gloves to meter out the coins, Shea hopped off the carriage.

"What do you have in mind?" Aidan called out to him.

"To talk."

The doorbell silver-chimed.

The main hall wasn't the way he remembered it: no more wheels under the ceiling—or ropes—no scent of resin and finished wood. No laughter; no clinking, somewhere in the corner, of beer mugs. People in white stood at equal distances from one another, each hunched over their own small table. Neat, clean, an invisible checkerboard.

A tall woman sailed up to him. "May I help you?"

"Good afternoon." Shea looked around, remembering. "I…"

"Are you here to order a dress?"

"No… Maybe. I would be interested in a guided tour."

"We don't offer tours, I'm afraid. But if you're looking to buy a dress, I can show you our fabrics."

"Sure," he said. "Thank you." *That door, across the hall. Still there. Here's hoping they hadn't tried to change the floorboards—*

"This is cotton with lozenges, and here's some striped linen. It's particularly beautiful with…"

There was zero chance they would get to the trapdoor with all those people around.

"When do you close?" Shea asked.

"…purple velvet. I beg your pardon?"

"When do you close the workshop?"

"At six. But it's still plenty of time to take your measurements if—"

"Listen, I've some money with me. I know it sounds very strange, but I assure you, there's no malicious intent involved."

"I don't understand."

"You just need to let me in after your close. I'll pay you whatever you ask."

"Let you in?"

Shea lowered his voice. "I won't take anything from the workshop. I'm not trying to rob you. I only require ten minutes ... I'll pay you, okay? I promise I won't get you into trouble."

She nodded slowly, staring at him. "Please give me a second."

A guy at one of the tables cursed loudly and puffed at his fingers—for a moment, that distracted Shea, and then the woman wasn't there anymore. When he caught sight of her again, she stood at the other side of the hall next to a bulky fellow with hands that, from the looks of them, could bend small trees.

Shea saw her say something and point at him.

Fuck.

The bell chimed again as he tumbled out into the street.

"Find out anything?" Aidan said.

"Found out we need to scramble, fast."

Rushing toward a back alley, déjà vu gripped him that he first couldn't place; then he remembered—*catch it, Danny, catch it.* The sudden influx of memory was so painful that he doubled over, palms on his knees.

Aidan interpreted this in his own way. "You should exercise more, my friend."

From the shadows, they watched the 'bouncer' step out through the front door, scan the street, disappear back into the shop.

Catch it, Danny.

"Let's forget the entire thing," Shea said. "Do you hear me, Aidan? Let's forget it and return to Owenbeg."

Aidan slowly turned his head and chuckled in disbelief. "What the hell is wrong with you?"

"Coming here was a mistake."

"Do you realize—damn it, I'm repeating myself—do you realize what's at stake? This is our future, combined. *And* the country's future—"

"No, this is your *belief.*" Shea pressed his back against the wall and slid down into a crouch. "Or Daelyn's belief. Against someone else's. You believe Duma would instigate a world war. The queen believes her legacy is a two thousand foot monstrosity. Drakiri believe that same monstrosity will bring about the apocalypse. One belief against the other."

"Except some beliefs have foundation in reality and some are pure superstition. What's the deal with the Drakiri, you said?"

"They're convinced..." Shea sighed. "They're *convinced* that once the tower is finished, another will materialize. They even have a name for it—the Mimic Tower. It's supposed to be a portal to hell."

"Surely you realize how crazy this sounds."

"Crazy, Aidan?" Shea glanced at him. "Same crazy as in 'devices we don't understand that can fly'?"

"That's different. That's technology, as opposed to superstition."

It was Shea's turn to chuckle.

"Look," Aidan said, "you have some weaknesses that would make it difficult for you to run the court, should all of this..." He raised his hands, palms up. "Should our plans work. You need to get rid of those weaknesses. Focus on the goal at hand."

Take the next step in the golden dance.

"I'm afraid we're out of options anyway—we can't get to the tulips," Shea said.

"Have you at least found out when they close?"

"At six."

"Then we're in luck, cause some of those bloody places stay open through midnight." Aidan turned around. "Let's meet here at ten."

"Where are you going?"

"You said thirty devices. We'll need help to transport them."

"How would we even get them?"

"Well, that one's pretty obvious," Aidan said. "We break in."

7

"Shea, wake up. Shea."

Hands shook him, disembodied hands, with no person behind them. He tried to free himself when things came into focus, arms appeared, then the face framed by strands of red hair.

Muriel.

"I had a nightmare," he said.

"Forget it. Look out the window."

"Let me just lie here for a few minutes."

"Wake up, something's wrong. I think something's happened in the city."

He sat on the bed, and a sickening feeling tapped on his abdomen. "Am I still sleeping?"

"What's the matter with you? Look out the window."

He did. It must've been seven or eight in the evening—he'd dozed for an hour, no more, and the void in his body left by the lovemaking had yet to close. In front of him, vineyards stretched down the hill's slope. A road snaked in the distance, and between it and the sunset orange of the river lay Oakville.

Against the darkening rim of the sky, a cone of purple light expanded from behind the roofs.

Give me time till tomorrow evening, she'd told him yesterday.

"What the hell is that?" said Muriel. "And what are you doing?"

He didn't answer, frantically trying to push his right foot into his pants.

The purple light boiled.

Heartbeat.

"I still think we should've simply smashed one of the windows," Aidan said. "Where did you learn to pick locks?"

"My sister taught me. She used to do it for fun when we were kids."

No questions followed: no *I didn't know you had a sister*, no *where is she now*. And anyway, in a few seconds, with a click, the front door opened into the transparent dark of 'Flying Tulips'.

"Shall we wait for your people, Aidan?"

"No, let's go in. They'll arrive in ten minutes or so."

Tables with fabrics heaped on them, clothing stretchers. A child's suit hanging from a coat hook. Shea had to remind himself why he wasn't a thief, why it was all warranted.

The door at the end of the hall drew closer, and with it, a vomit-inducing, ether-inhaling vertigo. There used to be a workbench here; Danny and himself had drunk beer over there. *You're fine, Danny, you're fine. Don't worry. You'll fit in.*

Voices in the street, Aidan's whisper: *Duck.*

Shea crouched behind a table, praying that the pile of cloth on it would be enough to conceal the top of his head. When the voices gained in force, he peeked over the linen waves.

A group of young people passed outside the windows. One of them, a girl, got close to the glass, either trying to look inside or examining her own reflection. A man laughed.

"Let's go…" Something loud and unintelligible. "Come on."

The girl leaned against the window with her palms. Darkness erased all features from her face, and moonlight went right through the hair. Shea imagined her lips moving.

The next moment, tiny purple garlands stretched among the shadows: Aidan pulled off one of his gloves.

More laughter. "…Let's go."

"Aidan," Shea whispered. "It's okay, they're leaving."

The girl pushed herself away from the window—but the garlands continued to shimmer until the voices outside became an echo.

Heartbeat.

The purple light boiled.

"Lena!"

In the square before the workshop—hands, more hands, tugging at his biceps, at the lapels of his suit.

"Get the fuck off of me." Shea slapped the palms and fingers away, shouldering his way through the crowd. "Lena! *Lena!*"

Of course she couldn't hear him. If she were even inside the workshop—he still clung to the hope that the mammoth vortex boiling purply toward the sky had nothing to do with her.

Maybe she'd gone to the vineyards. Maybe she'd gone for a drink.

The building loomed ahead, a shadow stretching over the centipede of the crowd.

He broke out into the free part of the square suddenly and unexpectedly, stumbling and almost falling. There was no transition, not a single onlooker left; ten feet before the front door, a dead zone started.

He noticed the details, the way the roof arched, as though crumpled by a giant hand, the way the windows curved inward.

Someone yelled, *Stop him*—and yet nobody did.

A second's hesitation was all he could afford. He raised his head. Somewhere above, invisible to him now, the purple cone swirled.

Shea stepped into the workshop.

Wheels and ropes, tangled into a nightmarish spiderweb. The wall opposite the entrance, grinning, and the wardrobe, no longer flying, squeezed into the hole.

It looked like something had tried to *suck the building in from the inside*, and from the ripples frozen into the ceiling, he gauged where this something was.

The epicenter lay behind the door at the other side of the hall.

Or rather, a door frame, a twisted and crippled one.

Heartbeat.

Aidan pushed on the doorknob.

It was a small room, twenty by twenty feet. Some shelves, brooms huddled together in thick shadow. Moonlight seeped in through the single window by the ceiling, reflecting off the lacquered floor.

"Okay, we're here, apparently." Aidan said. "So where are the devices?"

Shea tapped the floorboards with the tip of his boot. "We'll need a hammer and a crowbar."

"Or anything to tear apart wood. It doesn't have to be clean, you know. You go through those shelves, I'll look in the adjacent rooms."

Aidan's steps staccatoed through the main hall, and Shea swallowed the lump in his throat, wishing he could do the same with the fit of claustrophobia.

Forgive me, sis. I never wanted to return. But I need to see the dance to its end.

"I think this would do," Aidan said from the door frame, holding up an oil lamp and something that resembled a pair of goat's legs.

They worked in the jittering light like two coal miners, taking a pause each time Shea lost the grip or hit his finger—he could no longer feel his hands, heartbeat having occupied the entirety of his body.

One by one, the floorboards came off and the rosewood trapdoor emerged.

Aidan slid the crowbar between its edge and the floor.

"A hand here?" he said. "The damn thing's heavy."

Together, they lifted the door into an upright position. Underneath, a black rectangle gaped at them, all stale air and the reek of mildew. Shea put his foot on the first stair and thought, *help me, sis, help me save face, help me not to faint.*

"I can't see a thing." Aidan swung the lamp behind him.

"You will."

At this point, Shea didn't need light. He descended the staircase and took a few blind steps forward.

His hands found a lever and a valve.

Forgive me, Lena.

Then it occurred to him he no longer knew which Lena he was apologizing to.

The tulip hummed, rising into the air, painting the cellar in purple, rows upon rows of the Drakiri devices stacked on top of each other like wine barrels.

Aidan whistled. "Well, I'd be damned."

Heartbeat.

A twisted, crippled door frame. Past it, a small room, twenty by twenty feet. Good for keeping brooms in, good for indoor picnics.

The ceiling and the top of the walls had been torn off—a sculptor's mold of a closet, started, but not finished. At head height, a black egg hovered, wobbling and spewing purple light into the sky in a circular pattern.

Lower, soot covered the plaster where the two oil lamps had smashed into it.

Even lower lay the chairs with twisted legs—and the bodies.

Danny was dead, mouth agape in childlike wonder, skin on the right side of his face one big burn—he'd probably held a lamp when everything happened.

Lena's chest was still going up and down.

The only sound Shea could produce was a cawk. He fell on his knees, crawled up to her.

"Lena, Lena, Lena."

He stretched out his hand, then pulled it back, not knowing what to do with that broken flower of a body, whether to try and hold it.

She opened her left eye. "Shea. Danny... Where's... Where is he?"

"Sis, sis, lie still."

"Where's... Danny..."

"Danny's dead, Lena. Please, please." He touched her hair with his fingertips.

"Wanted... to teach him... show you how easy... that even he could use..." She coughed and spat blood.

Anyone but my brother, he remembered —and realized she could choke any moment. He gently wrapped his arm around her shoulders and pressed her face into his chest.

"You have to stop it," she mumbled. "Switch off... the device."

"Everything will be all right," Shea said. "We'll sit here for a while. For a little while. Everything will be okay."

"You have... to stop it."

"I have to, yes."

He never realized tears could flow uninterrupted, without beginning or end, the body simply fulfilling one of its biological functions.

"I love you, sis."

"Love you… too… brother."

With his boot, he pulled the remnants of the nearest chair under the tulip. Keeping balance atop that heap of wood proved difficult, but somehow he managed—maybe because he wasn't thinking anymore.

He screamed and fell when the black surface burned his hands. The device was red-hot.

"Damn you." He slammed his fist into the floor. "I don't have time for this. I don't have time for this."

When his palms lay on the lever and the valve again, he clenched his teeth and tried to forget about his skin melting away, turning and pulling through the pain's curtain, turning and pulling the way Lena did it.

The device shook one last time, spewed the last of its phlegm, and lowered itself onto the floor.

He smiled briefly. Chuckled. "I did it, sis. I did it."

There was no answer.

The people who found him—the ones who'd mustered enough courage to venture into the crippled building once the vortex had died—said he sat beside her body like a praying monk. He hadn't said a word, allowing himself to be brought to his feet, bandaged, and led out.

He didn't speak the next day either, or the day after. Only listened.

Heartbeat.

Heartbeat.

Silence.

8

Someone infantile had painted those trees and that morning light, someone who had just discovered whitewash and aerial perspective. In the same way, the sounds also lacked character: flat clicking of the horse's hooves, dry tapping of the three pairs of boots that flanked the cart loaded with dark eggs.

Aidan had hired some real goons.

He strode beside Shea, black gloves on, whistling something, visibly pleased with 'the catch'.

Pines squeezed the road on both sides. When a gap opened on the left, a trail behind a decrepit wooden gate, Shea said, "I need to take a detour."

"Pardon?" Aidan shot a sideways glance at him.

"The airship won't depart for another three hours. I'll meet you at the pier."

"As you wish—but try not to be late."

Shea hopped over the gate and followed the trail into the nascent day and along a cliff's edge. Beneath him, Musk Valley gained form, soaking up light like an orange sponge, white houses and mansions, tiny figures scurrying between rows of grapevine, preparing them for winter.

Morning sun always touched the Ashcroft estate last.

Between it and the vineyards lay something new, a small field of red flowers. Tulips.

He lowered himself onto the road. If he watched long enough and squinted hard enough, he thought, he would see a girl strolling among the flowers. He would wave to her, and she would wave back, inviting him in, telling him to come home.

When an airship crawled out of the clouds, still a distant and transparent contour, Shea got up and headed back for the main road.

9

Owenbeg greeted him with the same children slinging dust at each other, the same butcher in a stained apron, the same blind lattices of windows.

It felt like a different life—and maybe it was, everything alien, the castle, the battlements, even the tower. Events from a decade ago seemed more real than what had happened to him here.

In his quarters, he walked up to the glass-fronted cabinet. There were no golden lights in the reflection, no figures spinning in a grand waltz, only the desaturated monochrome of his own face.

Voices emerged from the courtyard: Brielle, talking to the people Aidan had hired.

Bring the devices to the tower, he mouthed what he couldn't discern. *Prop my tower up.*

As for him—he waited for Lena.

She came without a knock. She wore the same hunting suit as when they'd kissed for the first time, but she was even more beautiful, infinitely more beautiful now that he knew he was about to lose her.

He tried to imagine again riding with her in a caravan wagon, her standing in the ocean waves. Just a few seconds more in the world they never got, a few seconds before she speaks.

And she spoke.

"You piece of shit," she said. "What have you done?"

"I'm sorry." Shea held out his hands to her, then dropped them as he realized how pathetic he must have looked. "Forgive me, Lena."

"You've betrayed me. You little piece of... I'll tell the duke about our affair. I'll do it right away, and I really hope to see you hanging from the first tree they find for you."

"I had to do it," he said. "I love you, but I had to do it. If you believe nothing that I say, please, at least believe that."

"Love me? You think it matters to me, you think I cared for you? You think I care for you now? All those things I've told you about leaving Owenbeg with me—it was all a con. How could you be this delusional? I was using you, I didn't even like you, I was using you all along, as a collateral, as a backup plan in case the tower somehow survived.

"And now," Lena said, "I will destroy you."

The gulls went silent. The imaginary caravan wagon exploded just as Aidan's family carriage had.

A dark tongue licked the ocean waves away.

See Yaroslav Barsukov's story "Tower of Mud and Straw III: The Tulips" online at Metaphorosis.
If you liked it, leave a comment. Authors love that!
Remember to subscribe to our e-mail updates so you'll know when new stories are posted.

Copyright

Title information

Metaphorosis November 2020

ISSN: 2573-136X (online)
ISBN: 978-1-64076-181-0 (e-book)
ISBN: 978-1-64076-182-7 (paperback)

Copyright

Works of fiction

This book contains works of fiction. Characters, dialogue, places, organizations, incidents, and events portrayed in the works are fictional and are products of the author's imagination or used fictitiously. Any resemblance to actual persons, places, organizations, or events is coincidental.

All rights reserved

Moral rights asserted

Each author whose work is included in this book has asserted their moral rights, including the right to be identified as the author of their respective work(s).

Publisher

Metaphorosis
a magazine of speculative fiction

Metaphorosis Magazine is an imprint of
Metaphorosis Publishing
Neskowin, OR, USA

www.metaphorosis.com

"Metaphorosis" is a registered trademark.

Discounts available

Substantial discounts are available for educational institutions, including writing workshops. Discounts are also available for quantity purchases. For details, contact Metaphorosis at metaphorosis.com/about

Metaphorosis Publishing

Metaphorosis offers beautifully written science fiction and fantasy. Our imprints include:

Metaphorosis Magazine
Plant Based Press
Verdage

You can also find us:
@MetaphorosisMag, @MetaphorosisRev, @Metaphorosis
www.facebook.com/metaphorosis

Help keep Metaphorosis running by supporting us at
Patreon.com/metaphorosis

See more about some of our books on the following pages.

Metaphorosis Magazine

Metaphorosis
a magazine of speculative fiction

Metaphorosis is an online speculative fiction magazine dedicated to quality writing. We publish an original story every week, along with author bios, interviews, and notes on story origins.

We also publish monthly print and e-book issues, as well as yearly Best of and Complete anthologies.

Come and see us online at magazine.Metaphorosis.com

Metaphorosis: Best of 2019

The best science fiction and fantasy stories from *Metaphorosis* magazine's fourth year.

Metaphorosis 2019

All the stories from *Metaphorosis* magazine's fourth year. Fifty-two great SFF stories.

Metaphorosis:
Best of 2018

The best science fiction and fantasy stories from *Metaphorosis* magazine's third year.

Metaphorosis 2018

All the stories from *Metaphorosis* magazine's third year. Fifty-two great SFF stories.

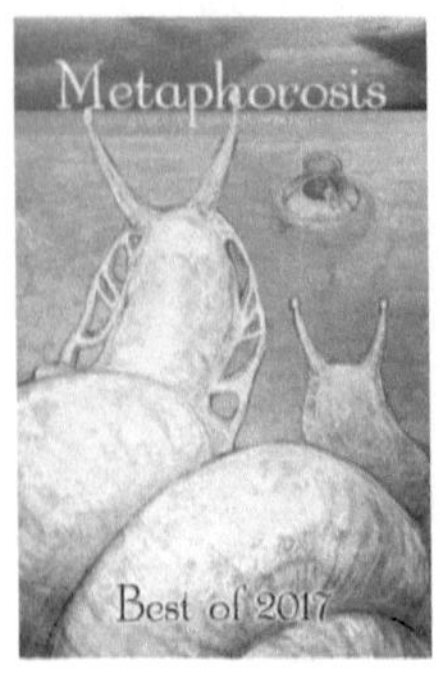

Metaphorosis: Best of 2017

The best science fiction and fantasy stories from *Metaphorosis* magazine's *second* year.

Metaphorosis 2017

All the stories from *Metaphorosis* magazine's second year. Fifty-three great SFF stories.

Metaphorosis:
Best of 2016

The best science fiction and fantasy stories from *Metaphorosis* magazine's first year.

Metaphorosis
2016

Almost all the stories from *Metaphorosis* magazine's first year.

Plant Based Press

Vegan-friendly science fiction and fantasy, including an annual anthology of the year's best SFF stories.

Best Vegan SFF of 2019

The best vegan-friendly science fiction and fantasy stories of 2019!

Best Vegan SFF of 2018

The best vegan-friendly science fiction and fantasy stories of 2018!

Best Vegan SFF of 2017

The best vegan-friendly science fiction and fantasy stories of 2017!

Best Vegan SFF of 2016

The best vegan-friendly science fiction and fantasy stories of 2016!

Susurrus

A darkly romantic story of magic, love, and suffering.

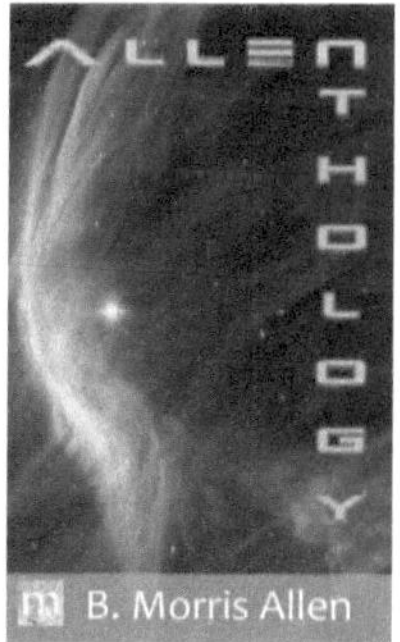

Allenthology: Volume I

A quarter century of SFF, including the full contents of the collections *Tocsin, Start with Stones,* and *Metaphorosis.*

Verdage

Science fiction and fantasy books for writers – full of great stories, often with an additional focus on the craft of speculative fiction writing.

Reading 5X5 x2

Duets

How do authors' voices change when they collaborate?

A round-robin of five talented science fiction and fantasy authors collaborating with each other and writing solo.

Including stories by Evan Marcroft, David Gallay, J. Tynan Burke, L'Erin Ogle, and Douglas Anstruther.

Score

an SFF symphony

What if stories were written like music? *Score* is an anthology of varied stories arranged to follow an emotional score from the heights of joy to the depths of despair – but always with a little hope shining through.

Reading 5X5

Five stories, five times

Twenty-five SFF authors, five base stories, five versions of each – see how different writers take on the same material.

Reading 5X5

Writers' Edition

Two extra stories, the story seed, and authors' notes on writing. Over 100 pages of additional material specifically aimed at writers.